Praise fc

'These are wry, disconcerting, ter.   a
restrained lyricism in the writing as we are plunged into these unwanted
lives. There's no set arc to these stories; they are melancholy and they are
very compelling.'
—Harry Ricketts, *RNZ*

'You will be dazzled by the discipline of a writer at the height of her craft,
where her words remind you that each sound, once spoken, becomes a
possible thing; that life is unreliable; the heart is indeed a muscle that
never stops twitching; and that in your place among women you will
always be warmly welcomed in.'
—Carla Donson, *NZ Herald*

'The collection focuses on relationships in a wry, somewhat cynical
manner that provides both recognition and humour for the reader,
and the author's talent as a poet is also in evidence in some impressive
passages. . . . Stories of this quality are a pleasure to read and I look
forward to more from this talented, often acerbic writer.'
—Owen Marshall, *Newsroom*

'*Bug Week* is an accomplished and entertaining read but one with an
emotional punch that belies its length. The latter stories in particular
signal with increasing force that for more than half of humanity, having
your life defined or rewritten by others against your wishes isn't a
metaphysical proposition. . . . This collection looks unflinchingly past
the illusions we have about ourselves.'
—Sam Finnemore, *Kete Books*

'One of the best works of fiction of 2020.'
—Steve Braunias, *Newsroom*

'In a collection of stories, the worries and niggles that press on the writer's
mind come through, sneaking and snaking through the characters and
the narrations, no matter how diverse. In *Bug Week*, these are clear –
our transgressions and our attempts to disassociate ourselves from the
natural world, love and sex, death and birth.'
—Josie Shapiro, *Read Close*

Bug Week
& *other stories*

Airini Beautrais

Victoria University of Wellington Press

VICTORIA UNIVERSITY OF
WELLINGTON
TE HERENGA WAKA

Victoria University of Wellington Press
PO Box 600 Wellington
New Zealand
vup.wgtn.ac.nz

ISBN 9781776563050

A catalogue record is available at
the National Library of New Zealand

Printed by Bluestar, Petone

for Michalia Arathimos

Contents

Bug Week   9

Living the dream   25

A pair of hands   32

Psycho ex   39

The baddest Toroa in town   48

The turtle   60

Billy the Pirate Poet   72

A summer of scents   93

The girl who shaved the moose   111

Sin City   122

Trashing the flowers   135

The teashop   148

A quiet death   169

Acknowledgements   181

Bug Week

At a certain age I began to think less about sex and more about tableware. I thought about wide-rimmed martini glasses and bulbous brandy balloons. I thought about crockery: matching dinner plates with small side platters and round soup bowls. I thought about the tinkle spoons make when stacked together and the subtly erotic act of sliding a perfectly sharp knife into a receptive knife block.

I dreamed my dreams in a home with scraggly wallpaper and peeling linoleum. At night I dreamed them in a bed that seldom stayed properly made, between pilling polyester sheets, next to a man with a balding ponytail.

Phil and I were not particularly wealthy. We partly owned a reasonable house. We had known each other for a long time and, having tangled and entwined year in year out, having created two curly-haired kids who often had sand or jam on their chins, the current lack of physical passion between us did not seem like so much of a lack. It was a reality I was unconcerned by.

Mine was the natural age of accumulation. My body was accumulating constantly and my kitchen cupboards were never stocked with the full complement of entertaining possibilities. My bookshelves, although groaning, spoke of need for shining covers closely pressed together, for beautiful colour editions whose prints seldom reflected light. The hot water cylinder whispered of linen and the pipes sang of the luxurious free-standing bath they longed to trickle into. Evenings and weekends I wiped cupboard doors and shined faucets, I laid shoes large and small in matching pairs by the door. I arranged fruit in my pièce de résistance, the cast glass fruit bowl – banana over orange, or orange against pear?

At work, Kelly, who was my age and should have known better, fantasised about people she wanted to sleep with. 'Last night I went into this bar and thought, Whoa, did I stumble in on a modelling convention?' she blurted. 'Every guy in the place looked positively Swedish.'

'I looked at a Swedish chair in a design store yesterday,' I said. I had looked at it, although I couldn't afford it. It had been plastic yet natural, modern yet elegant. It was made from a single sheet, with legs that bent back in perfect submission.

'I need a lover,' said Kelly, putting on her lipstick, or rather smearing it in the general vicinity of her lips, using the coffee plunger as a mirror. 'I so need a fuck.'

I have never understood people who apply makeup in company. 'Watch out,' I said, 'you could end up married or something.' It was perceptible that marriage and children were the things Kelly really wanted – and fast – fucks aside.

'Not necessarily,' she said. She smoothed her shirt and went back to her computer screen. 'It's the twenty-first century, and I was never particularly romantic.'

'Phil is trying to be romantic.' I didn't really want to discuss my personal life, but I felt it was expected. Suddenly the library catalogue in front of me looked very absorbing. Bug Week was approaching.

'That's nice,' said Kelly, with the hint of a question mark.

'He thinks we need more spontaneity in our lives,' I said. 'He's trying to be unpredictable. His hair keeps getting longer and it's driving me nuts.'

'Unpredictable how?'

'Oh, surprise picnics, random gift-giving. He's unpredictable in a predictable kind of way, if you know what I mean. Breakfast in bed.'

'I love breakfast in bed!'

'I can't imagine anything worse.' Crumbs get between the sheets, coffee gets spilled on the pillows. Grease is wiped on the bedside table. People who relish such things bemuse me. How is it pleasurable to wallow in one's own scraps? How does a devil-may-care attitude to cleaning lead to happiness? There is nothing romantic about filth.

'What else is happening in the bedroom?' Kelly asked.

'The bedroom is where we sleep.'

'Aha.' A knowing smile. Of course she didn't know. A welcome silence. Then: 'Does he ever break into song?'

'Not yet. I'm scared that one day I'll get home and there'll be an air ticket to Rarotonga sitting on the table, and I'll be expected to sort out my luggage in ten minutes, and leave without doing the washing.'

'Rarotonga!' Kelly said. 'Fucking hell, why wouldn't you want to go there?'

'Oh, you know. It's not that I'd rule it out forever, but I just wouldn't want to go at a moment's notice.'

Kelly shook her head. I have given everyone I work with a secret hairstyle nickname. Kelly is Hedgehog. Better, Albino Hedgehog – short, blond and spiky. 'I've never understood you,' she said.

I had to stop the conversation before she delved further. 'I'm going up to the bug room. Is there anything you need taken upstairs?'

I went up to the bug room, partly to get away from Kelly, and partly to spy on my colleague Don MacCreedy, the entomologist. Lately I had noticed that he was walking around in a state of permanent semi-sleep. His eyelids would flicker like he was on drugs; he would meander through a room and not see anything in it. I didn't know Don well but I had picked up a few things about him. He was able to focus intently, and while peering down a binocular microscope would enter a sort of trance that could last half an hour. He rarely engaged in conversation. On the other hand he was always impeccably presented, with crisp shirts, clean shoes and dignified colour schemes. He never wore the garish ties or revolting striped shirts that screamed, for some men, 'I'm going to WORK.' He shaved his face and kept his hair short and tidy, with no signs of a mid-life grooming crisis. People often infer that a well-presented man has a woman somewhere forcing him into it. However, Don lived alone. He was a divorcee and his mother was sufficiently ensconced in the Outer Hebrides to prevent her from ironing his trouser creases.

Don's appearance and behaviour were so anomalous as to be interesting. He was, I told myself, a rare genus I had yet to identify. I doubted the influence of substance abuse in his case, but I decided to keep an eye on him.

That day I arrived home with my heart in my throat, thinking about spontaneity. My one superstition is that saying things aloud can bring them into being. The table top was covered in bits of paper, which I screened anxiously. A picture of a giraffe by my son, Nicholas. A grocery receipt, two local papers, three empty envelopes and flyers for a Jamaican restaurant, a drycleaner's and a weight loss programme with a money-back guarantee. Last month's phone bill, some notes of Phil's, a couple of children's books from the public library and a copy of *Greatest Love Ballads arranged for Piano*, with an airbrushed rose on the cover. Part of my brain felt relief and another part quickly became absorbed in formulating the disappearance of the latter item. But fortunately the piano key was still hidden from the fourth birthday party.

'Darling,' came my husband's voice from the kitchen, 'how daring are you willing to be when it comes to pizza?'

Confrontation in a marriage is often best avoided. 'It's up to you, Phil,' I said, heading up the stairs. My mind raced with imagined horrors – steamed broccoli, pineapple, tinned kidney beans, crabsticks, piled into a cheesy mountain of unnecessary chaos. Fuck. I looked at the turned wooden stair rail and hated it. I thought about clean lines. I thought about ripping down the spew-patterned nineties curtains and I thought about minimalism, colours that were hardly colours. I went into the bathroom, wiped down the mirror, washed my face and thought about tiles. I thought of the tiler laying each one precisely, the years of development of the craft. Then I heard a familiar voice saying, 'Come on, it can't be that hard. I'll do it myself.'

'I just want some semblance of order in my life,' I said to my reflection. She blinked the water out of her eyes. She looked sullen, mousy and dishevelled.

I was enjoying myself at work one morning, making a dichotomous key for children to identify invertebrates. I thought about how everything in nature has a place, how everything is a component of a larger thing that fits into an even larger thing. I hoped the universe was like that, but infinitely. I thought about the mosaic vision of insects.

'You know what,' said Kelly. 'What'll happen next.'

'Next in what?'

'In your relationship. If things are stagnating or if neither of you are happy, one of you will have an affair. You will or he will.'

'I hope he does.' Someone else could be afforded the pleasures of R.E.M. piano renditions and jazzy shirt fabric.

'What about you?'

'I don't have time to meet anyone,' I said. 'Besides, I am completely unthrilled by the prospect of fornication.'

Kelly snorted coffee out her nose. 'How do you think of all the crazy shit you say?'

I pushed my glasses up my nose in a way I hoped was supercilious, and carried on with the *Guide to the New Zealand Forest*. Kelly was obviously reading lots of semi-teenage glossy magazines, or the type of novel that only sells because it fills the large vacuole in women's brains with sugary sustenance.

'Don the bug man has the hots for you,' Kelly said.

I felt a warm shudder go through me. It felt like the flu coming on. 'Bollocks.'

'It's true. He totally wants to fuck you. He's always coming in here and giving us stuff.'

'Kelly, in case you have forgotten,' I said, 'next week is Bug Week. We have twenty schools booked in to learn about entomology. He is a national expert.'

'Oh, how many beetle books do we really need?' Kelly has an arts background. I ignored her and thought about taxonomy. I thought about the beauty of phylogenetic trees. The thin calligraphic branches.

Later that day – perhaps this relates to my one superstition – a strange thing happened. Our office is opposite the lift, and as I went to shut out the draft, the lift doors opened. Don was standing in there, holding a stack of brown parcels. I thought of the tiny glass tubes that might be in them. Then for a split second he looked up. His long eyelashes lifted, the trance state wavered on the point of breaking. His eyes met mine for a brief millisecond and then looked down again. Janet from front of house walked into the lift, the doors closed, I went back to my computer, and a voice inside me said, 'That was the most erotic moment you have had in years.'

A song went through my body, not the kind that is sung but the kind that is felt, too low a frequency for the human ear. Sometimes distance is more intense than closeness. The knowledge that someone is thinking of looking at you, but deliberately stopping himself, can be a million times more provocative than any lover's touch.

At home Phil said, 'Honey, what do you think about Hawai'i this winter?' The Rarotonga scenario came back to me. My blood pressure rose slightly.

'Hawai'i is a long way away,' I said to my plate. Phil was experimenting with vegetarianism and had made soy cutlets. The children had used them as table scouring agents and most of their meals were on the floor. 'Where would the money come from?'

'Well, I figure it's such a horrible autumn this year, six more months of this can't be healthy. Why not have a week off in July and just let the bathroom renovations wait a couple of years.'

'I don't know,' I said. 'There is a mouldy smell in there. The whole thing needs gutting if you ask me.'

'Think of the kids with fresh coconuts, drinking the milk,' Phil said. His eyes were starting to twinkle. 'And we could see real lava.' The kids themselves did not look up. They were too young to have any concept of a planet or the Pacific Ocean. Phil shrugged. The twinkle died down. I could sense I was hurting him but felt too stubborn to stop. 'Just an idea,' he said quietly. 'Where would you like to go on holiday?' he asked Scarlett.

'Nana's,' said my daughter, adjusting her doll on her lap.

'Me too,' said Nicholas.

Their filial duty impressed Phil. I didn't want to mention the bottomless jar of jubes that Nana kept in her cupboard.

On the Monday of Bug Week, Kelly came in on tip toes. She uttered a few exclamations, then said, 'I got laid on Saturday night.'

'Really,' I said, no question mark.

'Guess how old he was. You'll never guess.'

'Seventy-two.'

She made a face. 'Twenty-three! Can you believe it?'

'I suppose so.' I have known twenty-three-year-olds to thrust themselves into inanimate objects while inebriated, but I thought better of mentioning this. 'Will you see him again?'

'Of course not,' she said, delightedly. Clearly she had already planned the next five years, the moonlit spa baths, the fireside sex, the declarations of eternal fidelity.

I knew the questions a woman was supposed to ask about such things. Was he any good? Did he have a big dick? How did it happen? Was he hot? But I couldn't face even polite enquiry. 'I'm going to get a cup of tea,' I said. 'Would you like anything?'

'Nah, I'm all right. I'll give you all the details when you get back.'

I didn't go to the kitchen. I went to the rooftop and looked out over the city. I felt high up and small and suddenly lonely. I thought about earthquakes and cloud formations. I thought of words like 'epicentre' and 'cumulonimbus'.

'I've never seen you up here,' came a Scottish lilt from a few metres away. Don the bug man had crept up on me. Or he had been there all along. 'I come up here about this time every day,' he said. It was before nine. 'Just to get some air.'

'Oh,' I said.

16

'I'm a creature of habit,' he went on. His eyes were fully open. The trance was momentarily suspended. I had the sense of a pond waking in the spring, shoots emerging from the mud. 'I like each day to follow a pattern.'

'Do you.' I couldn't breathe properly.

'Every morning I get up at seven. I have my breakfast at seven thirty. I get here at eight. I like to do my reading in the morning. I'm better at organising things after lunch. I always have about five cups of tea, at fairly regular intervals.'

'I like to eat breakfast alone,' I said. 'I get up early while everyone else is sleeping. I like to have all my clothes sorted out the night before, and I hang them over the end of the bed.'

'A sensible idea,' Don mused. 'I put on my clothes in the dark. I can't even see what they are.'

'I don't believe you.'

'Well, all of my clothes are much the same colour. As long as it's a shirt and pants I'll be fine.'

'Not enough people pay attention to colour,' I said. 'People think they understand it, but very few actually do.' I felt a little in danger of ranting but kept talking anyway. 'Colour can be overdone. Perhaps one small item of bright colour is enough, such as a scarf, or shoes, but the rest should be understated. The trees in this country mostly have small white flowers. If you look at the native forest, there is that lovely, soft, uniform green . . .' I could feel him watching me. 'I suppose I am talking shit,' I said. We had never had a conversation like this. I wasn't sure if the things we were discussing were entirely normal for acquaintances of our standing. 'I had better go back downstairs. We have a class arriving in half an hour.'

'Yes,' he said. He was standing closer to me now. 'Small white flowers with a pronounced nocturnal scent. Many of them are pollinated by moths or lizards.'

I risked looking at him. I hoped I didn't appear pensive or flushed.

'Admittedly I care about my clothes,' he said. 'A man who spends all his spare time scrambling up hillsides after insects shouldn't need to, but I do. I will only wear certain fabrics, for instance.'

'I am a stickler,' I told him, 'for cotton, silk and wool.' He nodded. We both stared ahead, quiet, unmoving. Should I stop there? Should I talk about the view or the terrible architecture before us?

'What kind of sheets do you sleep in?' he asked.

There was a sick, plummeting feeling in my abdomen. I coughed. 'Is that an appropriate question?' I asked.

'I'm sorry. I just believe that a lot of inferences can be made about a person, from these small details.'

I was already walking away. 'I would never sleep in anything but linen,' he said. 'Belgian linen. And it has to be white.'

Children chattered around me all day, made feelers out of pipe cleaners, cellophane wings. That evening I felt disorientated. On the way to the bus stop I walked into a shop outside of my budget. The blond assistant stared at my shoe hole, my wind-styled hair. Aggravated by her apparent deduction of my financial status, I walked out with an ostentatious paper bag containing a set of red wine glasses and a set of champagne flutes. I stayed up late at night removing tissue paper and standing the glasses on the bench, twirling and admiring them. Phil wasn't exactly furious about my purchases – fury was an emotion he never expressed – but he seemed morose. 'I thought we agreed we'd leave these things till the kids are bigger,' he said. 'That there's no point having fancy stuff with small children around.'

'I want my surroundings to be tasteful,' I told him.

'I thought they were.'

I looked at his fading Monet reproduction over the fireplace and was too tired even to scoff.

'You know,' he said, fingering the end of his ponytail, 'I think it doesn't matter what stuff you have or what your house looks like, if there is a loving family that lives in it.'

Something caught in the back of my throat. He was sounding a call to guilt.

'I don't want to bring up my family in a pit of squalor,' I said. 'I want to live in a clean house with smooth floors and curtains that aren't mouldy. I want a refrigerator that doesn't leak and a washing machine that doesn't sound like a jet plane taking off.' My voice was starting to rise, a thing I loathed in women. I cleared my throat and continued in a deeper tone. 'Yet you somehow insinuate that I am callous or shallow to want these things. There is nothing unreasonable about a few new glasses from time to time.' Phil was about to reply as I exited the room. I knew he would say 'But we have heaps of glasses already' and it would incense me too much to point out that not a pair of them was the same.

Don and I circled each other for the remainder of Bug Week, neither of us moving from our series of choreographed steps. I thought of the lyrebird with its tail over itself. I thought of the kākāpō, green in his hollow, of blue-footed boobies waving their oversized feet. I thought of stag beetles battling with their strange antlers. I pretended nothing was happening. Our conversations became shorter and more infrequent.

On Friday a teacher brought in a jar containing a bright green beetle, thinking one of her students had made a rare discovery. 'You can leave it here for our entomologist,' I told her. 'We'll get back to you.' Our entomologist replied to my email almost immediately. I was short of breath when I reached his floor, even though I had taken the lift.

Don was in a microscope daze and didn't look up when I walked in. 'Show us this beetle,' he said.

'You don't even know who you're talking to,' I told him. 'You have an eyeful of pond life.'

'I recognised the sound of your shoes.' The room was piled to the ceiling with filing drawers, each with a little pinned death inside. Don unbent from the microscope, took the jar and smiled. A joke I wasn't party to.

'People don't know their Coleoptera,' he said. '*Stethaspis suturalis*. This one is reasonably common in pine plantations and native forest.'

I wasn't concentrating. I touched his waist. I could feel warm flesh through his thin ironed shirt. This is not what you want, I told myself. You like neatness. You like distance. I pressed him against a wall.

'Let's not do this in here,' he breathed, close to my ear. 'There are one hundred and ninety years of collecting in this little room and I don't want to damage anything.'

'Okay.' I swallowed. I thought about how I could extricate myself. I thought of the antlion in its funnel of sand.

'Look, the mammal room,' he whispered. There were other people in the lab next door who may or may not have been aware of our presence. 'No one ever goes in the mammal room.' It was true. We never put the mammals on display because they turned people's stomachs. Most of them had mange; some of them had missing limbs.

'I'll meet you in ten minutes,' I said.

'This can wait. I can be there in five.'

In less than a minute we found ourselves in the mammalian

storeroom, in the controlled coolness between the tall shelves. A few hundred small glass eyes stared down at us. The smell of death, dust and preservation was overpowering. We couldn't touch each other.

'This is ridiculous,' I said, and Don agreed. 'These things shouldn't happen in a workplace,' he said. 'Come to my house tonight.'

'I can't.' I had two little heads to coax onto pillows. 'Some other time.'

'Will you kiss me?' he asked.

I looked up and saw the Tasmanian wolf looking back at me. Its lips were peeling. I couldn't.

Bug Week was over. The holiday in Hawai'i transmogrified into a week in Thames with Phil's parents. It worked out well for all of us. Phil enjoyed seeing his family, the children were content with the prospect of lollies, and I had a week at home by myself. It was luxurious. I cleaned and sanitised and ordered everything in my house, and then I went to Don's house at his invitation. We had sex a few times, which he seemed to find overwhelming. Afterwards he lay in silence with his hands folded on top of his chest, eyes unfocused. Don without his clothes was strange, pink and damp, like a peeled crustacean. I realised quickly that the desire I had initially felt had not been for him. I enjoyed his company, but it was mostly a necessary preliminary to spending time sitting on new leather couches, drinking decent wine, eating off flawless plates and sleeping between the aforementioned linen sheets. The sheets were always clean – it was as if there had been nothing bodily happening in them. I liked it that way. Don also had a slipper bath that one could slide into and remain slid. When I turned the taps with my toes to add more hot water, they made no sound. Afterwards I wrapped myself in huge thick towels the colour of stone. I saw my reflection in the large mirror over the basin. Her hair was damp and she looked older and less attractive than I felt. 'What are you doing?' she wanted to know. I couldn't tell her.

Don's house was sparsely decorated and completely compartmentalised. There were no hidden corners where dust could gather. There were no places to lose things. There was nothing burnt on to the ceramic stovetop. Nothing biodiverse lurked at the back of the fridge. The wooden floors shone and the ceilings were immaculate.

'I've lived alone for a while,' Don said. 'A couple of years, in fact. Shirley, my ex-wife . . .' He looked out the window. There was a view over moving trees and distant water. 'She was pretty unstable. When she left she trashed the entire place. Totally ruined it. That's why everything is new. She even ripped out the fucking plumbing.' A smile hovered on his face. Was it embarrassment or some form of humour?

'I can't understand how anything could prompt someone to do that,' I said. 'People do terrible things to each other but I can't see the point of getting that angry about it. I can't see how you could justify the waste involved.' Wine was making me talk.

'She was pretty angry, all right.' He put down his glass. 'I'm going to look in my cellar – would you like another drink?' And with that the book was shut. The story had been traced out but would not be embroidered. In some ways it was a relief.

'Something is going on with you,' Kelly said at work. 'You're even more agitated than usual.'

'I'm not usually agitated,' I said. 'And I feel fine. Nothing in my life is remotely different. Except I have a new dinner set.'

'You're a useless liar. Spill.'

'You make it up. I did whatever you think I did.'

'I know what you did,' she said. I knew she didn't, but part of me wondered if the Tasmanian wolf had been talking.

The week in Thames ended. The children came home and drew on the walls. Phil applauded their creativity and their articulation of their ambitions – Nicholas the future astronaut had scribbled a spaceship in the corner of the lounge. Kelly met a Spanish tourist with a beard and very little English, and came into work moaning that she was saddle sore. Don and I met occasionally for cocktails on Fridays, which could be justified as work drinks. Once or twice I let him caress my back on the rooftop. He was becoming reticent again: his eyelashes were beginning to droop. Soon he would either tell me we should cool it or tell me he loved me. I was afraid of both of these things.

One day I came home anticipating an evening alone. Phil had taken the children, along with his sister and her kids, to see some juvenile comedian. I put my bag on the hall table and walked into the kitchen.

It had been a mess when I left it, but what had happened now? Every plate – not just the new ones but every single plate – was in pieces on the floor. Every glass was smashed. The fruit bowl was in shards in the sink. I was too shocked to weep over it. My chest of drawers was emptied. All my clothes were off their hangers. The bookshelves had been disembowelled. In the bathroom all my makeup was emptied, scattered, smeared, strewn. In very small writing in dark grey eyeliner pencil the corner of the mirror read, *There is no order in the cosmos.*

'Who the fuck would do this?' I said. My heart was knocking around. I rang Phil on his cellphone – there was high-pitched laughter in the background. 'Phil, our house has been broken into,' I told him, voice cracking. He was genuinely horrified at what I described. Clearly he had nothing to do with it. Don was equally taken aback when I informed him. I rang Kelly just in case and succeeded only in disentangling her from Tomás and confusing her horribly. Who could have done this to me? Could it have been the resurfacing of the misfortunate Shirley? But she had long since moved home to Minnesota. I was sick with fear not knowing who knew enough about me to have made this melodramatic point. Would I be believed if the crime were reported? A garden variety housebreaker does not normally inscribe philosophical statements. Nothing appeared to have been taken. They will say I am nuts, I thought. They will say I have done it myself.

I sat on the bottom stair. I hated crying. I hated the trail of snot that slicked from my nose, I hated redness and swollen skin. I hated the small, timid sound of stifled sobbing. I thought about holding my husband. I thought about stroking the hair of my children as they fell asleep. I would replace everything exactly. I would put every book in its rightful place. No order. I thought about the honeybee doing its round dance and its waggle dance. I thought about the fish that home to the streams their parents came from, streams they have never swum. I thought about how our galaxy is spiralling around a fixed point. And then I thought of the atom and my head throbbed. The image of it whizzed before me. The electrons moved back and forth and filled up sub-shells. Their paths were impossible to follow. They were just a cloud of light.

Living the dream

When he arrived at work, Barry left his car and ran for the neighbouring horse paddock, a sweaty oilskin over his head and a pouch of tobacco in his pocket. He rolled himself a cigarette with numb morning fingers. Barry's life was divided between two places he was not allowed to smoke: the local high school, where he taught English and drama, and Arohanui Eco Community, where he normally resided. Sometimes, at home, he smoked in his car with all the windows closed while his neighbours sat around the rough-sawn communal dining table and talked, he imagined, about cancer. 'Breathe deeply,' Joyce the American yoga teacher would say to him when she had him captive on a rubber mat in the Lotus Lounge. 'Why are you always so negative, Barry?' Anna the robust Dutchwoman asked him at dinner. It was all very well for her to say, given that she spent all day around vegetables.

At seven thirty, Barry stubbed out the butt on a fence post that was ashed with several years' worth of his stubbed butts and walked calmly to the staffroom.

'Morning, Barry, how are you?' The deputy principal greeted him with the breath of a corpse, the product of coffee hitting a diseased stomach too early, a few red wines the previous evening and a lost toothbrush.

'Brilliant,' Barry replied as he scanned the room. Brian the librarian was reading the morning paper. Tina from science was eating microwaved porridge. As it was a Thursday, the counter was bedecked with decorated cupcakes: the anorexic economics teacher had been baking again for the starving children of Africa. A jar next to the cupcakes read *NO IOUs*. In a corner, Glenn the evangelical misogynist was talking to the wet-eyed student teacher from Auckland. Through her blond fringe her eyes showed genuine terror. Barry thought about rescuing her, but consoled himself by deciding that talking to him wouldn't be an improvement. He'd been assigned as her mentor but, despite her ridiculous beauty, he couldn't overcome his lack of interest in spending time with her.

At the bell, Barry was waiting in his chair. The three students who had arrived on time sat together, emanating awkwardness and speaking softly in a teenage language he didn't understand. A few more students arrived over the next few minutes, making as much noise as they could. Barry ignored it. Year Eleven Drama had a theoretical roll of twenty, but numbers fluctuated between five and twelve. Their work towards a production of *A Midsummer Night's Dream* was not progressing well.

As Barry handed out the scripts, Cameron Jonas moaned. 'Sir, why do we have to do some boring shit about fairies?'

Barry ignored him. 'OK, mōrena everyone. We'll try Act Four, Scene One to start with.' It was convenient that the four lovers were asleep at the beginning of this scene, as none of them were in class that day. 'Where's Oberon?' Yesterday Oberon had been Justin Marsh, who was playing rugby today at a school sports exchange.

'Sir, he's probably drunk at home,' said Jackson Whatu.

'Jess, can you read Oberon?' Barry asked.

Jess scoffed. 'I can't be Oberon, I'm Titania.'

Barry thought he heard Cameron whisper, 'He's been smoking his special tobacco again.'

'Guys,' Barry implored, 'we're supposed to be performing this in four weeks. Remember, this is for an assessment.' After ten minutes of arguing and protesting that they were there and it wasn't their fault, the players assumed a stubborn silence. Titania applied her lip gloss, glared at Barry, and began.

Year Nine English were kept in that morning because all the blue and red coloured pencils had gone missing again. Barry passed around an ice cream container and said, 'I'm not going to look, I just want you to quietly slip them back in.' The container did several rounds, slowly filling, before Barry gave up on the final missing red and let the students file out morosely. He was grabbing his banana and his keys and heading for the horse paddock when Sarah the student teacher appeared in the doorway, and he remembered they were scheduled for a discussion. Sarah would be teaching her first lesson that afternoon and was already squirming.

'Did you see that boy?' she asked in a horrified whisper. Barry smiled at her, perplexed. 'He had a giant purple bruise around his mouth.'

'Oh, yes – Tom,' Barry said. 'Don't worry about him. It happened in my class on Monday. Kharma Te Rangi took my coffee cup and told him to suck it onto his face for as long as he could. So he did.'

'Oh.' Sarah blushed. The redness deepened until her hair seemed like snow and her eyes shone bluer and bluer. Barry decided that he wanted to sleep with her. He looked at the cuffs of her grey silk shirt and thought about the tiny wrists beneath.

'Here's my lesson plan,' she said, handing him an A4 sheet. Everything was neatly arranged into boxes titled Topic, Learning Outcomes, Links to Prior Learning and so forth.

'Oh, training college.' Barry sighed. He began to read

aloud, partly out of habit and partly to embarrass her further. 'Year Twelve English,' he read. 'Topic: "The Scarecrow" by Ronald Hugh Morrieson. Activities: Think/Pair Share ten minutes. Character role play twenty minutes –'

Sarah interrupted him. 'I was thinking, to make it fun, I could get them to imagine they were the characters, and have a conversation. Like, pick any two characters and talk to each other. You know, about what they're thinking and that.'

'A-ha,' said Barry with a smile.

'Do you think it will work?' As she looked into his face for a sign of approval, he realised she was serious. He wanted to say something cinematic, like, 'Honey, let me tell you a few home truths.' He wanted to say, 'Whatever you do, so-and-so will sit there gazing at herself in a compact mirror. Such-and-such will be drawing male genitalia in the back of his book. What's-his-face will have the appearance of intense concentration, but only because he got stoned at lunchtime.'

He said, 'Sure, it'll be fine.' He made some half-hearted excuse involving photocopying. He was desperate for a cigarette.

Sarah's lesson didn't go as badly as Barry had expected. He sat at the back of the room behind his cluttered desk, where he normally never sat. He looked at the blue training college form he was supposed to be filling out and lost concentration. His stomach was audibly rumbling. He'd only had one sandwich for lunch and half of it was crust. Every week Barry made five loaves of wholegrain bread by hand, kneading the dough with more a hatred of humanity than a love of wheat. And every week the loaves were quickly disposed of down the gullets of his neighbours and the tourists from Willing Workers on Organic Farms. It was the beginning of peak WWOOF season, which meant an influx of virile Germans, space-cadet English girls on a world tour of spiritual and sexual experience, and South Koreans from the cities who carefully pulled out vegetable seedlings and left the weeds. Last night he had been lying in the outdoor bath when he'd been chanced upon by a WWOOFer woman who was wandering through the trees in a dirty white dress, like a shade. She'd sat beside him and talked for a while, oblivious to his slack nakedness, unconcerned about his hairy chest and bald patch. She'd offered him a toot on a green glass pipe, which he'd accepted. He'd wondered if she might climb in with him. He was still considering what could have happened as he watched Sarah testing all his whiteboard markers. Upon finding one that worked, she began to draw a map of character relationships. Her trembling hand made a spidery two-way arrow linking Prudence and the Scarecrow. 'So, how do you guys think she feels about him?' she asked. The room fell silent at last, and remained that way for a painful number of seconds. Then Kim Walker said, 'Um, like he's an old perv and stuff.'

Barry remembered the floral-sweat scent of the WWOOFer's dreadlocks. When he was just starting to enjoy her company, she'd said, 'You must be pretty happy here, living the dream.' Then he'd asked her to leave him alone.

'How do you think that went?' Barry asked Sarah after the three-twenty bell.

Her crimson colour returned. 'OK,' she said. She adjusted her armful of books and added, 'To be honest, I felt like a complete fool the whole time.'

Barry's cue had come. 'You know, when you're a teacher, that feeling never really goes away.'

He'd found out she was staying at the Watson's farm, which was only a couple of k's from Arohanui, so he offered

29

her a ride. He regretted it as soon as they drove out the school gate, her in the passenger seat where chickens sometimes roosted. He realised that his car was filled with dropped nails and bits of rope, and had various scrawled reminders stuck to the dashboard. It was the Ford Falcon of a madman. It stank of tobacco and the spilling of secret beers (Arohanui was also dry). They rounded the fern-dripping bends of the one-lane road; they saw the odd sheep picking its way through the scrub. 'This was my dream once,' Barry said, confusing Sarah and the dreadlocked girl in his head. 'A bit of land, planting trees, working with kids. Trying to change the world for the better.' Sarah didn't say anything in response. She was gazing out the window with the wistful expression of a girl who is thinking about a very, very attractive man who happens not to be there. 'I started out teaching in South Auckland,' he went on. 'In some ways that was even worse than up here.' He laughed. 'Had a knife pulled on me once.' It didn't matter that she wasn't listening. He was talking to someone who wasn't talking over him. 'I could write a book about all the things kids have called me. You learn to ignore it.'

Sarah got out at the Watson's gate and said goodbye courteously. Barry watched the breeze lift her skirt, exposing the backs of her knees. Following his earlier decision that he'd like to sleep with her, he made another, more noble decision not to act on it. He waved to no one and turned the car around. But he didn't go straight home. He parked by the estuary and sat looking at the muddy tide, fiddling with his keys in his lap. He watched the pied stilts standing nonchalantly on one leg. He thought to himself, If I have to spend one more day in that shit place I am going to freak out. If Joyce talks to me one more time about homeopathic remedies for smoking cessation I am going to scream. He saw a heron lift itself out of the water and thought, If I drove in there, would anyone notice? At low tide the estuary mud was bejewelled with the roofs of abandoned vehicles. He thought to himself, I live in a land of immense natural beauty and incredible human stupidity. He tried to breathe deeply but didn't enjoy it. He returned the key to the ignition.

A pair of hands

Richard and Helen had lived in the town nearly three months before they discovered the park by the river. Only a few blocks' walk from their rental, grass grew wetly in the shade of exotic trees. Adjacent to the children's playground with the giant octopus and the concrete mountain, the paths and glades seemed like a fantastical garden. They had intended to drive further to find a picnic spot, maybe south to the wild beaches cut up by quad bikes and the wind. But a bent palm tree beckoned them like a long ridiculous finger, so they parked up, spread their tartan blanket and unloaded their rustling shopping bag of cheese, fruit, bread and carbonated drinks.

'This is beautiful,' said Helen, looking around, plastic knife in hand. 'I wonder if anyone ever comes here?'

An hour or more passed and they didn't see a soul. Occasionally, sounds came through the trees – the high-pitched calls of small pirates capturing invisible ships. But there were no footfalls, no barking dogs; no one disturbed their idyll by the water.

'It's about time we got to know the river,' Helen said.

The river swamped the heart of the town, chewing its soft banks, picking logs from its teeth. Around the bridges the river moved almost silently, that massive body of water with its inhuman might. When Richard looked down on it, his skin tightened. The river still received raw sewage from the town, and from the hills it wound through it brought farm effluent, dead trees and tonnes of eroded soil.

'I'm so glad we moved to a town with a river,' Helen added. She was on one of her positive spins. Like a moving candle, Helen cast an ever-changing light over the facets of her life. She would wake early to prepare for her nursing shift and say to Richard, 'You know, the good thing about my alarm waking you up, is that you can hear the dawn chorus.' The blackbirds sounded their clearest, sweetest notes, and Richard felt harassed. The same Helen would come home in the late afternoon, slump at the table in her uniform, look at Richard reading the paper, and say, 'Didn't you find a job today?'

Richard was not lazy: he was orderly. In the mornings he liked to rise at a regular time: not before eight. He liked to drink two cups of tea, the second stronger than the first, while he read the front page of the paper and the classifieds. The situations vacant were few and unpromising. The main street was flecked with empty shops, dust crusting their windows. At the end of the river the downgraded, dying port sat like a scab, silting up, sealing the town's former exit. In the local factories, machines came to a final halt. Business shuffled elsewhere. Richard would close the paper with a sigh and set out for his morning walk: to look at the water, to see what the town had coughed up. In his walks around town he discovered a range of things. In the local museum he looked at photographs of colonial dreams: white frock photographs, steamer photographs, photographs of new tram tracks and shops with names like 'Drapery'. He found out that they used to call the river the 'Rhine of the South'. Perhaps, he reasoned, in hope of recreating a Europe that even in Europe no longer existed. He found it interesting that the restaurants, shops and warehouses sat with their backs to the river. It was as though it were something filthy that no one wanted to acknowledge was there.

At around noon he would have his usual lunch of either baked beans or eggs on cheap, thin toast. He would eat this in the company of the National programme, staring out the ranchslider at the flat green square of backyard. He imagined himself growing borders of marigolds and curly parsley, picking sprigs to decorate his eggs. He imagined himself making great sculptures, centrepieces for sprawling estates and public parks. More than anything he wanted to work in marble, carve classical folds of cloth, curlicues, smooth white hands. He knew it was old fashioned. After lunch he carried out whichever household chores seemed urgent, and then returned to the paper to read the middle. That was where Helen usually found him.

Their picnic came to a natural end. They crumpled the bread bags and slurped the last of their drinks. They tried to be mildly intimate on the picnic rug, but the pressure of their bodies made mud ooze from the ground. The rug was not large enough for them to stretch out, and they soon became uncomfortable searching for ways to extend their legs without wetting their feet. Helen suggested they take a walk, so they wrapped the rug around their rubbish and clicked it back into the car boot. Arm in arm, they wandered under the shade to the riverbank, Helen pressing her head into Richard's shoulder. At that time, twelve weeks into their new life, they still held hands in public. Helen felt a rush of contentment and desire at the smell of Richard's woollen coat. His fingers felt smooth between hers. She tried not to think of them as the fingers of a man who did not work.

The driftwood lining the riverbank was bone-like, holding bottle tops and dead pens in its grip. That year, the river had spilled into the lawns and low-lying lounges of their suburb, leaving an icing of soft brown mud. Helen made a cake to commemorate it, adding instant coffee until the right colour was replicated. Baking was one of the things she made up her mind to. Every few days she made up her mind to do something. What I really, really would like to do is sew a dress – a dress for parties! I can see myself holding a glass, in this fabric. What I want to do is go for more long walks, explore upriver, buy some proper boots. What I am determined to do is be kinder to Richard. I will look for his good qualities and praise him for them – then he is bound to pick up. I would like to start amateur theatre. Sometimes I wish I had studied drama instead of nursing. Somehow the made-up mind always left a loose thread, which eventually unravelled the whole thing. As they were walking, Helen made up her mind to come back here, to this park, to this riverbank, perhaps after work some days, perhaps with Richard, perhaps alone.

'What's that smell?' Richard asked. His nose was a source of personal pride. This river, in spite of its baggage, tended to carry an earthy scent. But this scent was very much flesh – a dead bird, maybe, a fish disembowelled by the tide.

They kept walking, shoes scuffing the wood, vaguely curious, mostly unconcerned.

'Remember the seal we saw at Paekākāriki?' Helen said, thinking of their latest discovery of death, a furred tragic pungency, and then –

'Oh!' Helen inhaled the sharpness of shock. 'Oh, oh, oh, oh!' She started to dance from foot to foot. In spite of all the gruesome things she had seen at work, this, this was –

'Hands,' said Richard in bewilderment, a sense of wonder creeping over his immediate fear. They were whitened by water and he thought again of marble. The skin was bluish, like the de-fuzzed skin of a possum he had once seen in the creek of his childhood. Their severed ends were wiggly – lobes of fat, dangling tendons. From one of them a bone protruded, round and yellow. A carpal, Richard told himself, and somehow this word was reassuring. They were hanging out of a plastic bag – it was silly, really; it had acted as a flotation device and brought them here rather than the riverbed, where they must have been intended to rest. This was the act of a dumb criminal, Richard decided. But who, while disposing of dismembered body parts, would be thinking straight?

Helen was still hopping about. 'Shit, shit, shit,' she whispered. 'What do we do?' For once, it appeared to Richard she was relying on him: to take the lead, to guide the situation, to solve the problem at hand. A new thread of pride wound into his mind. His stomach churned like a bucket of punch. 'We've got to tell the police,' Helen said.

Richard stood there calmly, looking across the water, which was turning grey as the sun clouded up. 'I'll wait with the hands,' he said. 'Just in case they wash away. You go and phone the cops.'

'I didn't see a phone booth anywhere around here.'

'You'll have to find the nearest house and knock on the door. Go to one of those houses over the road from where we parked.'

Helen started to walk away, and then paused. 'Richard,' she said, as if the hands were listening. 'Richard.'

'What?'

'Don't touch them, will you? Whatever you do, don't touch them or move them.'

'Of course not.' And Richard stood and watched the hands, stuck in their nest of sticks, grisly yet peaceful, the rigor of death in the looseness of life. He thought all the logical thoughts:

36

Whose hands were they? Where was the rest of that person? Who would do such a thing? Why would they do it? And then in turn he thought of logical answers: It was gang related. It was drug related. It was a family dispute. There'd be a body in a gully somewhere, a shallow grave in the bush. A sharp knife had been used, but not that sharp. They'd probably been chopped quite recently. Skin breaks down remarkably quickly in water, and these hands still had a good coating of skin.

It seemed like hours that Helen was gone. When she returned, a stocky man in blue with a set, unsmiling mouth was at her side. A few paces behind them walked a woman, brisk and neat, armed with a clipboard and camera. Helen had waited by the car for the police to arrive and was guiding them to the site, highly agitated and talking excitedly. The officers looked at Richard a little strangely, then introduced themselves, shaking his hand. The man's palm was warm and firm.

'Okay,' said Richard. 'What happens now?' He heard the crackle of a walkie-talkie.

'We'll need to ask you a few questions,' the woman said.

More police arrived and unrolled tape. Richard and Helen answered all kinds of enquiries, from their names and address to the contents of their picnic. Their statements gave the time of discovery, their exact location, the method of discovery.

'How long have you been waiting with the hands?' the woman asked Richard.

'I didn't mind too much,' he said. 'I thought if a kid came along, or something, I could warn them.'

'Thank you,' the stocky officer told them. The shadows of the trees were lengthening. 'We'll handle it from here.'

Was it a pun, wondered Richard – had he said that on purpose? 'Will you let us know what happens?' he asked, and the cop gave him that strange look again.

'That won't be necessary, sir.'

He imagined himself reading about it in Monday's paper. It would probably be front page. He would be eating his breakfast while he read about it. The journalist would mention him and Helen. Then he would turn to the classifieds and see if any decent jobs had come up that week. While he read the ads, he would still be thinking of the hands.

Helen was hysterical all the way home. The hands had opened up all kinds of closed lids in her. 'I still feel sick,' she wept.

What I want more than anything, Richard was thinking, dreaming of stone and a chisel.

Psycho ex

I am going for a run. I pull on my leopard-print tights, my black sports bra, my hot-pink singlet; zip up my hot-pink jacket. Shoes, a little worn and in need of replacing. Which footwear manufacturer is the least evil nowadays? I lock my back door, slip the key into the little pocket on my hip. It presses into my skin like a secret.

I am not going up, or anywhere near, Mount Victoria.

So I head up the hill away from the stretch of shops, because uphill is where trees are. I'll maybe turn right at Coromandel Street, go through the town belt around the back of the zoo, check up on the baboons. They always seem so happy in the early evenings. They eat grass and murmur to each other: *wurg, wurg.* There's the alpha male with his harem of females from just-post-pubertal to peri-menopausal. There are the young males watching for an opportunity. Then there's the old guy, used-to-be-alpha, sitting off to the side with just one loyal mate left, running her fingers through the few remaining hairs on his head, looking for lice. I reckon she was his first love, and the one who's stuck by him. I believe in love. That's what I'd see if I ran that way. I pass the bus stop and the traffic's busy, so I don't cross the road. I head up Alexandra Road instead of Coromandel Street. I can run over to Hataitai and still technically not be going to Mount Victoria.

The path takes me through the trees. I watch my leopard legs flashing over the grass, the dead brown pine needles. I imagine myself as a leopard, running through a forest, powerful, unafraid. You always said I was too colourful. You complained so much about my purple stonewash jeans I gave them to the op shop. Then we broke up. I wish I'd kept the jeans. I'm nearing the lookout now, the weird triangular sculptures. The trees open up, give way to sky. The sky's turning pinkish. You can't beat Wellington, even on a bad day. But Wellington may beat you.

I'm dropping down from the lookout, re-entering the forest. Like entering a bedroom. But I'm single. Yep. All the single ladies. Waving my hands in the air halfway between freedom and desperation. The hill gets steep here; I have to brace my knees. I'm keeping myself alive, I tell myself. My joints, my tendons, my muscles, my heart. The heart is a muscle that never stops twitching. I'm going down the concrete steps, and I'm on your street. But I'll pretend I'm not: I won't look at your house. The psycho ex. The stalker. That is not who I am. I am simply a person who loves you, loves you deeply. I have never felt this way about any other man. I feel like Wanda Jackson, down down down into the funnel of love. The thing about love is that it isn't insane. Love is the purest, sanest thing any of us will ever feel.

A light's on in your lounge, and there's her head in the big picture window. She's on the couch, reading or something. Checking her Twitter. No face visible, just her golden head. Your golden girl. You married her after about five minutes, but it still makes perfect sense to me that she was the one you'd been looking for all along. She's naturally blond with enormous boobs. I have no boobs, like literally an AA cup. It's useful for running – I don't even really need a bra. I just wear one because I feel like that's what one ought to do. No boobs, and I always hoped you were an arse man, because my arse is all right, running is good for the glutes, but I always knew deep down you were a boob man. When we were having sex I used to imagine myself as someone else, a big-boobed woman. Probably younger than I am, with fantastic melons that had sprouted out of my chest and not yet felt the effects of gravity. The way they'd bounce. The way they'd fly, wildly, as you hammered me like crazy from behind. The way they'd rock as I rode you. Whenever I came, I came to myself. I hadn't been me, and then I was again. It was like you had never actually fucked me.

Your street is also steep. I cross the side roads – whoever thought of laying out a square grid on the side of a mountain? I get down to Kent Terrace, pant at the lights. Back up around the Basin, past the seedy pubs on Adelaide Road, the hospital where I was born. Get home, my one-bedroom flat, see my work piled up on the kitchen table. You'll be having dinner, sitting opposite her, talking about your respective days. I'll be eating with work. I turn on the shower, hear the drops hit the steel tray, peel away my sweaty clothes. When I see steam rising, I step in. I have the water so hot it almost cooks me. Saltiness runs down my face. I scream at the showerhead like it's a cruel god.

I am going for a run. I am not going up, or anywhere near, Mount Victoria. I say this to myself every evening, like a spell against . . . what? How more cursed could I be? I'm already screwed. I go for runs, I take the meds that mean I can't even wank. Love is the only medicine. Love and seawater. If it's true you're married now, and it is, all I can do, all I can do, is find someone new. The best way to get over a guy is to get under

41

the next one. But – under? Does it have to be under? Can't it be – I don't know – sideways?

The neighbour's cat watches me as I stretch my quads, my hamstrings. 'I know, I'm nuts,' I say to her. She squints and looks away. Cats know everything. They look into your face like you're the simplest mess. I don't have a cat. A single woman without even a cat. It's really just me. I shouldn't feel sorry for myself. I should get out more. I should – I don't know – join a club or something. Or take up a martial art.

But which martial art? Which one would best enable me to kick your bastard arse? Which one would have me prepared, knowing exactly which direction the next blow would come from? My heart's been broken over and over. I really thought you wouldn't. I thought I was old enough now that this would be it. Like, enough smashing myself up against brick walls. Enough flogging dead horses. Look at the lights of the capital slowly blinking on, a whole fucking city of dead horses. There ought to be a martial art for the emotions. How to fight with just your heart.

This evening I see her walking around the lounge. She's tall, a little heftier than I am. Top-heavy, like she could topple forward. Bounce back up on her big rubber boobs. She's arranging something – well, why wouldn't she, it's her house, after all. It was your house, that house I spent so many nights in, in your room with the tapestry wall hangings, rocking in your arms like a small boat on a gentle sea. I know every washbasin in that house, every inch of carpet, every shelf, each room's wallpaper. She'll be changing things around. She'll have replaced your old brown Temuka with whatever crockery she's into. Wedding presents. I wasn't invited, but a friend showed me some video footage. It was all so strange: her in white, you in a suit, when all you ever wore was corduroy pants and a hippy shirt. Why did you do this? Things had got shit at work, I went to India for two months and meditated and ate fruit, we agreed to go on a break. And back from the break, you'd got engaged. She was a Trump refugee. She predicted the outcome of the election long before anyone else. When he won she was out of there like a flash. Married you to stay in New Zealand. That was her, but why did you do that? Were you mad at me for leaving? You know I meant to come back. Did you marry her to piss me off?

Do you still love me? I still love you.

Love is the purest, sanest thing any of us will ever feel. Love is not crazy, not manipulative, not needy. It just gives and gives, like a dripping tap. Like a broken tap the water's gushing out of. Where can I get a plumber for the emotions? Who can stop up this awful wastage?

I wasn't going to slow down. But it's getting dark: she won't see me. I just want to sit for a while, to be close. You don't have a fence, just a ngaio hedge. The leaves contain a natural insect repellent. There was that time, I can't remember which time or where, but somewhere near Nelson, I think, we camped in a ngaio grove, and you rubbed leaves onto your skin to keep the sandflies at bay. We ate rice and lentils for dinner and porridge with soy milk for breakfast. The tent was a small and joyful room where we made love over and over, our sounds travelling around the mostly empty campground. It was just before Christmas. Which year was that?

The dead leaves crackle under my butt. I'll pretend I've dropped something. I don't wear a Fitbit, but say my Fitbit has fallen off. I know they're designed not to. I've worn it out though. I am really, really fit. I crawl on my hands and knees, feel sticks pressing through my tights (galaxies today), and get to the other side of the hedge. I look up to the warm light pooling around the lounge window. I think I can smell Nag Champa incense, but maybe it's just my imagination. I think I can smell chai.

Suddenly it's all her, all five foot eleven of her, taking up the whole window frame, her face sort of glowing. She's seen something moving. She's seen me! I'm over the gate. I was good at hurdles. I hear the front door click, hear her accented 'Hey!' Does she know it's me? Does she even know I exist? Did you even tell her when you married her that you'd left a relationship of five years to be with her? Five fucking years.

I don't turn around. I keep sprinting ahead. I've never gone this fast downhill, and I'm scared I'll go flying, land and flay myself on the tarmac. I can't breathe. I can't breathe.

I am going for a run. I am not going up, or anywhere near, Mount Victoria. I put on my mermaid tights, my royal-blue merino singlet, my brilliant aqua jacket. I am a sea creature dancing in an ocean of twilight. I am a bird of paradise twirling through the trees. Why is it that with birds it's the males who are beautiful? Why do men expect women to be beautiful, when they can have pot bellies, hair in their ears, turn up to a party in their trackies. The care I'd take coordinating everything, wanting every day to be lovely. To be manicured, to smell good, to never let a long black hair grow out of a mole, to never fart. My mother with her dry dyed hair, with her grim mouth, with her crack-filling foundation. I don't want that to be the story. I met you and I thought we could start at the very beginning. Back before the apple. All the stories, fixed. Romeo and Juliet but not dead.

But you killed it as casually as one might an ant.

I'm at the lookout, with the wind beating my head. Clouds moving in, faster than clouds ought to. Wellington beats me.

The whole awful place. Fuck this place, this city that's broken my heart over and over. I'll go back to India, travel up through Nepal, find God in the mountains. I'll go to Australia, pick pineapples or something, instead of staying here in my one-bedder with my proper job. My proper, awful life. Now there's no you, no settling down and starting a family, what is the goddamn point of pushing paper, having a reliable pay cheque. Life is unreliable. If only there were emotional pay cheques, if only fortnightly the heart could be topped up. Here you are heart, another two weeks of bliss.

I can do a longer run tonight, cut down to Balaena Bay, go around the waterfront towards Kilbirnie. It'll get dark before I'm done, but I'll stick to the footpaths, keep out of the town belt with its gnarled tracks. Who would even care if my throat was slit? How many days would it take people to work out I was missing, that I might have died, before strips of me were unearthed by someone's curious dog?

So I come out of the trees, and I'm tired, and your street's the quickest. She's suspicious since last night. I can't risk it again. Lights are on, there's no one in the window, maybe she's in the kitchen or the bathroom. You might be home or you might be working late. If I could get round the side of the house without anyone seeing I could check for your bicycle. I could just know if you were there or not, I could stand on the footpath pretending to be catching my breath – as if breath was what I was chasing all that time – and I could breathe in the night air that held the closeness of you. Close to your neighbour's fence the ngaio are shaded. I have dropped an earring. I am creeping. Creepy. This is creepy of me, it isn't normal, it isn't sensible, it isn't done. People at work would not do this. Most people would not do this. There's a crackle of windblown junk mail under my hand. I'm through the hedge.

I'm on the path down the side of your house, the familiar concrete pavers surrounded by loose pebbles, the familiar slightly peeling weatherboards. Old house, old town, old hopes, old dreams: I can't stomach it.

The back door clicks open, there are footsteps. Someone taking the recycling out. I'm a possum in the headlights, the security-lit path with the next-door neighbour's fence on one side and the wall of your house on the other, both unscalable. I hear her voice saying, 'Hey Tom, there's someone here again.' I hear your voice answering from inside the house. I hear her say the word 'police'. Fuck. I do the dumbest thing. I run down the path, past the lean-to where you keep your bike and a few garden tools, jump your currant bushes, scramble over the wall to the back neighbour's section. The neighbour's curtains are drawn. Oh, God. My heart is going to pop. If I can get out of here, out onto the next street over. But there's a movement behind me, someone's coming over the wall, I hear the scrambling of limbs. I run like a stupid rabbit, darting whichever way to elude its pursuing fox. Where is the street? I leap another fence, crash through bushes, parkour over a garage, I can't find a way out of all these twilit yards. These houses are so close together. I hear a dog barking. Oh, God. I fall, and there's mud and I'm bruised and I'm crying. I am sitting on a heap of something. There's a faint smell of rotted orange rind. I crawl forward in the growing dark, my body shaking, sobs unable to be stopped. My dog – I'll say I'm looking for my dog. I make it to the front of a house where there's a low wall topped with a picket fence. I climb it crying, get a picket point right in my mermaid cunt. I sit down on the footpath sobbing and shaking some more. I feel a hand on my shoulder, feel the warmth of a body settle down beside me. I couldn't shake you off.

'Come here,' you say to me. 'Come here.' And you pull me close to you and hold me in my aqua iridescence, in my compost stink. You don't ask me what I'm doing; you don't tell me off. You knew all along it was me, all those times. You were waiting for the chance to catch me at it. I don't need to explain myself. I'm sobbing against your chest, and you're holding me close, soothing me, stroking my back, my hair. We're sitting on the footpath in Mount Victoria, a street over from yours. I hear traffic but I don't make out the shapes of people or cars through my tears. My eyes are walled up. What I am thinking is, you and I are like those baboons, the old man baboon and the old woman baboon. No matter how many wives you have, I'll always be your first wife, the one who never stops loving you. You've never held me tighter. I have nothing for you. I have nothing to say to you. You say nothing to me. When you have finished holding me, I will get up and walk away.

The baddest Toroa in town

I knew him from somewhere. I saw him walk into the pub ahead of me, black shadows around his eyes, shit in his tail feathers. He looked like he'd just come back from several weeks at sea. The pub was full of people in a similar situation. Some of the big trawlers had just changed shifts and here we were, washed up again, with that strange feeling in the legs you get back on dry land. After many nights of enforced sobriety, most of us were headed to the Stubborn Oyster.

I'd had time to get home, have a shower, wash off the stink of fish, eat a pie out of the freezer. I didn't bother getting dressed up. No one in that town ever did. If you wore long pants everyone thought someone was getting married or had died. There was no dress code at the pub excepting some ancient notice forbidding motorcycle helmets and baseball bats. All the women wore flannel shirts or Swanndris, had their hair cut to a couple of inches. You never saw cleavage in that town. Only at Roxanne's Massage Parlour, and then it was likely to be covered in scabs and bruises.

Scrote – my workmate at sea, flatmate on land – was already seated at the bar and had saved me a stool. I see that man so often, sometimes I think if I die in a place where Scrote isn't, I will die happy. But I was content to take my place next to him, exchange greetings of familiar obscenities. Seeing that big black-and-white bird walk in had put me on edge. He was seated over by a window by himself – not drinking, of course. I knew what he was, Toroa, but I wasn't sure where I'd seen him, why I felt like we'd met. I couldn't get rid of the feeling that he was staring at me.

The league was on but I didn't care about either of the teams. It was more a background hum of commentator drivel, a blue and yellow blur moving across the field. After the game finished, Jono went and switched on the microphone and adjusted the stand, and we settled into the usual Friday night routine of music and spoken-word open mic. People did a wide range of stuff there. A guy with a waist-length mullet would play metal-inspired guitar solos. Baldy sometimes told dirty jokes. A woman who skippered a cray boat sang ballads. We occasionally got guest musos from other towns.

A nervy Christian couple from Gore got on stage and sang some folk songs, him on guitar and vocals, her on the zither. You could tell they were Christian by the frequency of the words 'God', 'Lord' and 'Jesus'. Folk and blues have a lot of that, but there comes a tipping point. We get along all right with God down here, but we don't always like to be reminded about him. Particularly when it's Friday night and our objective is immobility.

The woman had greying brown hair in two pigtails. He was big and meaty in the head, like someone who holds his breath too much. 'What's the bet he goes home and fucks her up the arse,' said Jono from behind the bar, moustache bristling.

I decided that everyone was drunk enough now that I might get up and recite some poetry. They put up with that here. They call me Bryce the Bard. I've gone from being an oddity to a regular spectacle. I wrapped my hands around the mic and began:

The sea, that old salty whore
Lets down her thick kelp hair
Rolls and lounges on the shore
Under the twilight's pall

And the drunken sailors
Singing at the toothless moon
Shake their heads, say, 'Boys, it's soon
She'll have us, hearts and all.'

And every time I leave
the sureness of the dock –

'If I might interrupt,' came a voice from the throng. It was him, the bird. It was a rasping, hissing voice, a voice without teeth, a voice that water might have.

I protested. 'I was just getting to –'

'Whaddya think he could have rhymed with "dock"?' called Jono. 'A-ock, bock . . .'

The bird flapped up and perched on the stool behind the mic stand. He was enormous. I moved out of his way. When he spread his wings, all three and a half metres of them, the wingtips hit people. His eyes were glinting. I could tell he was angry.

'I came from the sea today,' he began.

No one was surprised by this. At the arse end of the world nothing shocks us. We had a bull elephant seal come ashore once and hump himself over Mrs Hobson's fence. He lay in her front garden for a week and flattened her succulents. All he wanted to talk about was his sex life, how many cows he'd fucked. He was filthy.

You have to understand that not only was everyone drunk in

that town, everything there was drunk. Telegraph poles leaned drunkenly in the wind. Cars came drunk around the coastal road. Around the wharves, seagulls vomited up their breakfasts. Every hairdresser, every lunch bar, every sporting goods store was like walking into a hangover. If it wasn't drunkenness it was something else. Nothing fazed anyone in that town.

'Most of you are fishermen,' the bird continued. 'Now, I don't have to tell you that the sea is changing. You have seen it yourselves. Fish don't school in the places they once did. Clouds make abrupt turns over the water. Currents are moving differently.'

At first the noise didn't abate. People shouted their conversations and heckled the bird the same way they did any open mic-er. Someone, in a moment of confusion, yelled out 'Cock-a-doodle-doo'. The bird ignored everyone and spoke louder. I wasn't sure if the sound was coming out his beak, or if he was somehow booming it into our brains.

'I've been around nearly sixty years,' he said. 'Soon I'll die. When I come in to land it's on an island some way south of here, with good strong winds and beautiful cold weather all year round. Every two years I've built my nest from tussock and sods of earth. My mate has laid an egg and for eighty days we've sat on it. When the chick hatches we feed it for another eight months. Now you may have heard that albatrosses mate for life. I have to say that isn't entirely true.'

Here we go, I thought. The elephant seal all over again. But he went on, 'I've had two mates. The first one died after two chicks. Drowned on a tuna line. The second lived until recently. Now I am too old to mate again.'

'Never say never,' said Ginger Tom, who was sitting in the front row. A few of the older men in the room looked a bit droopy in the mouth.

'Of all the chicks I've hatched, how many are alive today? Probably none. Some were eaten. Many made it to sea but died out there, caught on hooks, got tangled in nets and cables. Anyone here worked a tuna boat?'

A few of us raised our hands.

'I don't have to tell you how those long-lines work. Out behind the boats for miles, shorter lines clipped to the long one, a hook on the end of each, er . . .'

'Snood,' I said. 'They're called snoods.' He raised his beak at me. 'But it's mostly purse seining,' I added quietly. We'd look for a school then wrap the net around them, close them in, drag them on deck in tonnes. I've never liked the tuna work. The big ones have sometimes got to be clubbed to death. They can slash you to buggery, those fish.

'They bait the hooks with squid,' Toroa said. 'Squid is one of our main food sources. We also eat carrion, crustaceans and salps.'

'What's a salp?' someone shouted.

'A planktonic tunicate,' said Toroa.

'What's a tunicate?'

He seemed to wince. 'Oh, never mind.' How little we know the sea. How many small and wriggling things live in there that we can't name, that we hardly look at. 'We can't see those lines underwater. No one could. Squid is getting hard to find. The boats go where the birds are feeding, that will be where the fish are. We end up taking the bait. We get hooked, through the beak or eye or through a leg, and drown down there if we can't get off. All through the sea there is less and less squid. Even the sea lions are starving. I never thought I'd enter a plea for those egg-sucking . . .'

'Bastards?' suggested Ginger Tom.

'Those bastards are dying,' said Toroa. 'In nets, and from

starvation. Tens of thousands of albatrosses die in the Southern Ocean every year. Most of my chicks. I came here today, from the sea, to ask for your help.'

No one was heckling now. We watched him, some frowning, some blank.

'There is nothing else I can do. I am asking for your cooperation. You must stop plundering the oceans.' He sat there on the stool, challenging us with his great pink tube-nose.

The muttering and murmuring started up again. 'Don't blame me, I'm in oysters,' said one guy. Another stood up and pointed at Toroa. 'That's not even a real bird,' he said. 'Some fucking greenie dressed up as one. Fuck off.'

I was in front of this guy, and elbowed him. 'He is a fucking bird,' I said. 'Don't make him mad.' A few people looked at me like I was nuts. Others looked down at their gumboots.

'Mate,' said Scrote eventually, 'we've gotta eat too. Some of these guys have families. They have to feed them. Fishing is just a job, mate. We don't set the quotas. We don't make the rules. Me and him' – pointing to me – 'we just drag in the nets. I hardly ever saw a seal in one, or a flippin' dolphin or whatever.'

'Why don't you go up to the Beehive?' Baldy called out. 'And while you're at it, tell those cunts to put some proper roads in around here.'

'There's nothing any of us can do,' Ginger Tom said. Many concurred.

'Talk to your mates,' said Toroa. 'Talk to your captains. Talk to the boss of whatever company you work for. Tell them what I told you.'

But why us? I wondered. Why come here, of all small towns? Why this particular pub? Sure, it was closer to his island than some places. But you get a feeling, at the arse end of the world, that no one even knows you're there, let alone will listen to you.

People were grumbling now. The bird had thrown a gloom over the evening. No one wants to be asked to do something on a Friday night. No one wants to be told his way of making a living is reckless and irresponsible. Sometimes a band has to stop playing while the audience breaks up a fight, and tonight it felt like that. The party was over.

'Have it your way,' said Toroa at length. 'Don't do anything. Keep setting the lines. Keep dragging in the nets. Keep chucking us overboard. Don't log us. But in your lifetime, very soon, you will see more changes. And what you see will be worse than anything you could ever imagine.'

He flapped down onto the floor, was lost from view. I thought he would probably storm out, but instead he padded up to the bar, hopped onto a stool a few away from where I'd reseated myself. Jono must have felt sorry for him, because he offered him a bowl of deep-fried calamari chips. The bird spat in disgust. Jono just shrugged, found some raw squid in the kitchen and passed him a bucket of it. Toroa sat there, gulping it down.

Although I didn't say so to anyone, I regretted not finishing my poem. I felt that it was some of my best work. There was no point in reading it now. Everyone was looking maudlin. Ginger Tom tried to sing 'Unchain My Heart' into the mic, and someone kicked the stand away from him. There was a screech of feedback. At the bar we were all helping empty the whisky bottles. Stuff that had sat there for years because no one had a taste for it was now being socked back. Some of it was probably quite good, but we wouldn't have noticed.

I realised nothing was going to come of the evening, and left by myself.

All the streetlights had gone out. Some drunk fuck had hit a power pole, no doubt. I walked home by moonlight. There seemed to be two moons, which shifted in and out of each other. I found myself rhyming 'ocean' with 'emotion' and 'notion'. It was pointless. It was a shit poem from the start. Who was I kidding? I was no bard. I was no visionary. I was just a washed-up deckhand who drank too much, who'd just hallucinated that a bird had come into the Stubborn Oyster and told everyone off for catching too many fish.

When I got home I sat at the kitchen table and stared for a long time at the salt shaker and the dirty plates. I always found it hard to sleep, the first night back on land. At sea, lying in your bunk, you're always listening with your body to how things are moving. Sometimes the water calms; the ship just sits there; you could be on a bus or sitting in front of your telly at home. Sometimes you hear the great steel carcass clank and groan, sounds that seem to resonate from deep within the ocean, kilometres down.

Scrote came in through the back door, crashing and swearing.

'Scrote,' I said to him, 'I've been thinking. We're going to be twenty-seven this year. We've been on those boats nearly ten years. I'm starting to think I'm ready for something new.'

Scrote and I had been to school together, and after spending our final year sitting daydreaming, our too-big legs barely fitting under the desks, we spent a season picking apples in Golden Bay. We did hops for a while, then kiwifruit. One day we were in Nelson hanging around the port and chanced upon Nate from school, who was working as a deckhand. He said you'd be at sea for long stretches and the work was hard, but the pay was great and you got a good amount of time off. Plus, he liked being out on the high seas, away from everything. 'Have you ever been somewhere you can't see land?' he asked us.

Our first job was in an on-board factory, filleting hoki. No drugs or alcohol on board, they told us. We thought they were joking. After the first hangover, breathing fish guts in the early morning, it started to make sense. There were a few of us new guys. One was seasick the whole trip, talking of nothing but getting home. One wanted off because he missed his girlfriend. We were merciless with this unfortunate Romeo. 'For fuck's sake,' said Scrote, 'just have a wank, and imagine she's doing the same.'

Most of us got nicknames on that first trip, or maybe the second. Scott became Scrottum, then Scrott, then Scrote. I was the only one who got called by my name. I was envious at first: the granting of a nickname seemed like a badge I hadn't earned. Now I don't mind that I don't have to introduce myself to strangers as an aspect of male genitalia.

'Bryce,' Scrote was saying now, 'I don't want to hear about all your life's problems. If you've got any weed I want to hear about it, but otherwise I'm going to bed.'

'Nup.'

He walked to his room, muttering. 'Think I'm happy?' I heard him say. 'What the fuck else is there to do? Think I'm happy living in this shit town, drinking in that shit pub with no nice-looking girls and a fucking bird comes in and rants at us? I'm going to bed by myself . . . millionth fucking time.'

'So there *was* a bird,' I said to the Formica. I thought about what it would be like to work with mussels or crays. Buy myself a bit of land somewhere and grow a few things. Go to a place where more people lived, where everyone wasn't drunk and animals didn't talk; meet a nice girl. It was slim pickings on the boats. There was a pretty one who worked in the factory of the last ship I was on. All I could think about once we got naked was the amount of guts she pulled out every day. You never get that smell off your skin. Underneath whatever cream or perfume she used, it was always there, the metallic whiff of blood, the vomit tang of a fish's half-digested lunch.

I woke in the late morning to a tapping at the window. I knew who it would be before I pulled the pillow off my head. My window was rusted shut. If he wanted to come in he would have to come through the front door like a civilised person. I put on my boxers and a singlet and went to open the bolt. He nodded at me and walked straight down to the kitchen, where Scrote was burning bacon.

'What's that fucking bird doing in here?' Scrote shouted. 'It's gotta be bad luck or something to have one of them in your house.'

'I think it's only bad luck if you shoot one and hang it around your neck,' I said.

'Huh,' said Scrote, burning himself some toast.

The bird and I sat at the table. I couldn't offer him a cup of tea so I didn't make one for myself. My brain felt like it had been soaking in a whisky vat all night. We didn't have any fish in the house, either. For about the last five years I hadn't eaten a scrap of it.

'Why did you come here?' I asked Toroa.

'I told you last night.'

'Nah,' I said, 'I mean, why did you follow me home?'

'You have to help me,' said Toroa. 'You are a poet. Write a big, long poem about the sea.'

'I feel like it's all been done before.' Scrote's breakfast was making me nauseous.

'Do it again. It's probably more effective than writing

57

letters to politicians.'

I didn't have the heart to point out that neither of those things made the blindest bit of difference.

'I've seen you before,' I said. He didn't say anything. I had an image in my head of a big albatross floating on the water, resting, waiting. A snow of white across his folded black wings. I'd had the feeling he was eyeballing me. But when was it? I'd been to sea so many times, seen any number of birds. Sometimes we'd see a whale spout, or its tail thwack the surface. I had a recurring dream about being eaten by a sperm whale. I'd always thought of a seabird as a good omen, but maybe this one wasn't. Maybe he'd make storms come, maybe he'd put a curse on me and Scrote and all the other guys, and stop us getting laid for another ten years.

'I've told you, I'm old,' he said. 'I'm tired. I don't want to tell my story again. You know what I've talked about. Just write something. I don't care what it is. Write anything. Get it into print, or go to every pub in the country and read it to people.'

'Want any eggs?' Scrote asked me.

'Not in front of him,' I mouthed, pointing at our guest.

'I have to go,' said Toroa. 'The wind is picking up. I can get good lift from the top of this street.'

'I might see you again,' I said, 'somewhere out on the water.'

He said nothing in response.

I let him out the front door. I got a pencil and turned a grocery receipt over to the blank side. *He spoke to me of salp and snood*, I wrote, but didn't get further. I went to the lounge window to see what he would do.

The bird spread his great wings and ran down the road. His big grey feet slapped over the tarmac. Halfway down he lifted off and headed over the last two blocks towards the sea.

How do I begin to tell his story? A southern royal albatross walks into a bar. Stallion of the high seas. King of Campbell Island. The meanest black-eyed bird in the sub-Antarctic. The baddest Toroa in town.

The turtle

Dionysus is hiding in the bushes. Althea can see the curl of his hair, the jut of his chin, between the leaves. Her feet, in their school shoes, feel heavy as she nears him. Her breathing changes. A flicker of nervousness swirls around her heart and in her gluteal muscles. She concentrates on looking straight ahead. There is another boy with Dionysus, the usual one who wears too much hair product. 'Show us your tits,' one of them shouts as she passes. 'Come on, don't be shy.' The two of them burst into laughter. The gelled boy's laugh is a guffaw, whereas Dionysus makes a pleasant sound. It isn't fair, thinks Althea. Something so stupid and ignorant in such beautiful packaging. It isn't fair that despite this daily harassment she feels tender towards him.

Philistines, she thinks. Her jaw is locked with humiliation, her feet keep moving forward. Feet can generally be relied upon, even if faces can't. Althea doesn't know what a Philistine is, but she likes the sound of the word, with its hard 'ph'. His name isn't really Dionysus.

Dionysus is the first person who has made Althea think of the word 'fuck' as a verb. In part of her brain, some primal part, she wants to have sex with him. Beginning as a six-year-old child, Althea has put herself to sleep every night by imagining herself in romantic situations. Up until recently, all these imaginings have culminated in a cinematic kiss. Meet me by the tōtara tree at a quarter to nine . . . No, he wouldn't know it was called a tōtara. Meet me under that big tree at a quarter to nine. The sky is deep blue. An owl hoots softly. Their lips meet . . .

But now with Dionysus, known to everyone else as Damon, Althea imagines she is taking her clothes off. That they are taking their clothes off, throwing them around the room. There is his naked body, just as she has imagined it. How his warm skin would feel. How wet she would get. Her hands, caught in his curls. His teeth.

Althea's mother, Rosemary, is sitting at the dining-room table, fingering the hem of her skirt. She recognises her daughters by the sound of their shoes, knows this is the oldest one without turning around.

'It's a quarter past four,' says Rosemary.

'I had a meeting after school,' says Althea, truthfully. 'For orchestra.' She puts her clarinet case on the shelf by the door.

'Have you seen or heard from your sister?'

'No.' Althea and Phoebe avoid each other at school. 'She probably went to a friend's house.'

'She hasn't replied to any of my messages. Do you have any idea which friend?' Rosemary gets up and paces the kitchen. She has made afghans today. Phoebe's favourite. Althea likes Anzac biscuits.

'Nup.'

'Excuse me?'

'I mean, no, sorry Mum, I'm not sure.'

Althea walks to her room, dumps her bag, changes out of her school uniform and into a T-shirt and trackpants, goes to the bathroom and splashes water over her face. In the kitchen she selects a biscuit and pours herself a glass of milk. She considers asking if she can have an iced coffee, but Rosemary is clearly in a bad mood.

'Did you have a nice day today, Mum?' Althea takes the walnut off the top of her biscuit and eats it separately.

'Oh, it wasn't too bad. I took Gran to the bank.' Rosemary is fretting. 'I'll ring Georgia's house first,' she says, more to herself than to Althea.

'I had an OK day. My maths test wasn't too hard.'

'That's good,' says Rosemary. 'Ella, or perhaps Sophie, are the other main possibilities.'

Althea sits down at the piano. She gets out her Debussy book and presses the pages back. Mum is walking around the room with the phone held between cheek and shoulder. She gives Althea a look and points to the phone sharply. Althea fingers the keys. You can press them down all the way without making a sound, if you press them slowly enough. The little hammers touch the strings gently. Sometimes there is a slight hum.

'OK,' Rosemary says into the phone. 'I'll try Ella.'

She rings the parents of five girls. The fifth one is Min's mother, who doesn't speak English, but she puts Min on the phone, who tells Rosemary that Phoebe was last seen at twenty past three, leaving the school gates to meet her boyfriend at the park. Althea knows about Phoebe's boyfriend, who has existed for several weeks already. But every time she hears the word uttered, she feels a tightening in her chest.

Rosemary knows the boy is called Jayden, but cannot bring herself to utter his name. 'She has gone to the park with that boy,' she says. She rakes her fingers over her scalp, pulse racing, stomach churning. Then she turns to her older daughter. 'It is very likely that your sister has become sexually active.'

Althea slumps onto the piano and begins to cry.

Phoebe walks slowly to the park. She doesn't want to get there too early and seem too keen. She stops outside the dairy for a couple of minutes. If anyone sees her standing there, they will just think she is waiting for a friend who is inside. There is a message from her mum, but she will answer it later.

Jayden is waiting on a bench near the children's playground, hands deep in his pockets, back bent, headphones in. He stares at the ground in front of him. Phoebe doesn't think he is particularly handsome, but she likes the sulky shape his mouth makes when he is thinking. If he thinks, that is. Phoebe isn't sure if boys really do. If you ask one what he is thinking about, he will just say 'I dunno' or 'Nothing'. Georgia found Jayden for Phoebe. Unattractive as he is, he will have to do, for the time being.

'Hi,' Phoebe says. Jayden doesn't look up. 'What are you listening to?' She stands in front of him, holding her schoolbag straps.

'Hey,' says Jayden.

'What are you listening to?'

'Korn.'

Phoebe laughs. 'That's pretty old-school.' She sits down beside him, spreads out her fingers on either side of her. Phoebe doesn't believe in ingratiating herself with boys. She isn't going to pretend she likes Korn too. If this boy doesn't like her, there are others.

'I brung my turtle to show you,' says Jayden. He pulls a little oval shell out of a pocket in his bag. When he puts it on the ground, a head with red cheeks, and four tiny legs emerge.

Phoebe can see the turtle's neck pulsing as it breathes. 'Can he live out of water?' she asks.

'Yup. He can live in the water and on land.'

'What does he eat?'

'He eats turtle food.'

'What's that, like meat and stuff?'

'I guess so.' Jayden kicks at the asphalt. He is wearing enormous sneakers with their tongues hanging out. They aren't school uniform. Jayden says he doesn't give a shit about school. Phoebe knows why. Jayden can't read.

'Let's see if he'll eat some grass,' Phoebe says. She is going to be kind to Jayden. He can't help it if he's dumb and a little bit ugly. Phoebe has always empathised with the underdogs – the kids who still drooled when they were ten, the ones with funny haircuts. Phoebe is in the accelerate class at her school, but all the boys in that class are dicks. Matthew Grady, for instance, has already joined the Young Nats. Oliver Simpson says he is going to be a famous writer, and he says he has written three novels already, but he can't even spell 'inconvenience'.

Phoebe tickles the turtle's head with a blade of grass, and the turtle ignores it. He looks so sad. 'What's his name?'

'Bert.'

'Bert the turtle. Why did you call him that?'

'I dunno.'

Bert the turtle just sits there. Phoebe taps his shell, but nothing happens. 'Put him on the lawn and see if he walks around.'

Jayden lifts the turtle up, thumb and forefinger on either side of his shell, and places him on the grass. Jayden's hands are big and calloused. His nails are short and stumpy, and all around them the skin is ripped and scraggy. Phoebe wonders what Jayden does all day.

Bert still doesn't move. 'I think he's scared,' says Phoebe.

'I'll put him back in my bag,' says Jayden. 'Wanna go for a walk?' He picks up the turtle again, slides him tenderly into his backpack's rear pocket. From the front pocket he takes a packet of roll-your-own and a lighter.

'You know that will kill you.' Phoebe smiles.

Jayden just shrugs and smiles back. He already knows how to roll cigarettes like an expert. He licks the paper so quickly, seals it shut. Phoebe imagines him working in a factory, licking cigarettes closed.

'Can I roll one?'

'Thought you didn't smoke.'

'Oh, no, I don't. I just want to learn how to roll them, that's all.' Phoebe likes to learn new things. You never know when a skill might come in useful. You might be in an earthquake and there might be a smoker trapped next to you, with both their hands under the rubble, and they might really need a cigarette, just to help them through. Jayden shows Phoebe how to lay the tobacco along the paper, how to leave a little gap and fit the filter in it, how to roll the whole thing between your fingers until the paper curls up. Phoebe's cigarette looks precarious and lumpy. Jayden sniggers. 'It looks like a spliff,' he says. Phoebe has never smoked marijuana. She supposes she will have to, eventually.

They walk through the park, side by side. They don't hold hands or anything. Last week, Jayden gave Phoebe a hickey. It was covered up by the collar of her school shirt, thank goodness, but she was worried about it at home. She could have worn a scarf, but it's summer, and she never wears scarves. Mum would have known. Phoebe took a bottle of foundation from the secret makeup kit under her bed and carefully sponged it over the mark. She was proud of the way it blended in with the rest of her skin.

Phoebe and Jayden walk for a while, then sit by the pond. Jayden gets Bert out again but is worried he might run away and jump in the water, and he'll never find him. They talk a bit. Phoebe does most of the talking, asking questions, and Jayden gives her short, unpretentious answers. They get up and walk again, and when they get to the road, Phoebe says, 'I better go home. Mum will want me to help with dinner.'

'OK,' says Jayden. 'See you.' He gives her a hug and kisses her on the mouth. Phoebe has been disappointed by kissing. It's not at all like in the movies. It's wet and sloppy, and you can taste someone else's breath.

Rosemary is throwing the afghans into a tin with horses on the lid. There's no one she can talk to. Her mother, tacked on to the family in her granny flat, doesn't really count. Whenever Rosemary asks her for advice, all Vera says is, 'Oh, I don't know, dear. That never happened to me,' or, 'You were a good child. You never did things like that.'

Rosemary fits the lid on the tin and squats down to check the casserole. Rosemary has never owned a car. She walks the couple of blocks to the supermarket, carries her groceries home in home-sewn reusable bags. All her clothes are handmade. She makes everything by hand: biscuits, crackers, bread, pastry, pasta. Butter and cheese from raw milk a friend delivers. She buys organic when she can, and avoids plastic, but it's expensive eating well. She hasn't got back into work since the girls were born. It's hard for any mother, but nearly impossible for a sole parent. She would have stayed married if their father hadn't gone off with that woman from work. She was always clean. She kept her hair long. She made love to him whenever he wanted, including lunchtimes, sometimes, or early mornings when the girls were still asleep. Even though she didn't really enjoy it. She'd never figured out what all the fuss was about. A man heaves away, squashing you into the

66

mattress, squirts in you, and you have babies. You get slim again, you pluck your eyebrows, you pay attention to colours. He starts coming home with an odd smell, smiling differently, his mouth lifting up on one side. You keep lying back and letting him but he leaves anyway. The children scream a lot. They have nightmares. They won't sleep in their own beds. They go through mountains of mince, acres of school uniforms. You pay for piano lessons, drink hot water with a splash of milk to fill up your stomach. They get to teen age and behave like a pair of ungrateful minxes, tell you they hate you, blame you for everything. Rosemary knows she has to protect them, but sometimes she wants to send them far, far away. Somewhere like a boarding school, with horses. If only she had any money.

It is some relief that Althea feels as upset by the thought of underage sex as Rosemary does.

Althea sits on her carpet, legs tucked up against her chest, and stares at the wall.

She has a large collection of candles, given to her at birthdays and Christmas. All together, they have an overpowering scent, like overripe fruit. Althea likes to read by candlelight. Sometimes she puts a candle in the middle of the floor and watches its light flickering on the walls. Sometimes she writes a name on a piece of paper and holds it in the flame, watches smoke curl up. It never works.

It is completely untenable. Phoebe is fourteen and already having sex with boys. Althea will be seventeen in a few weeks' time. She has never been kissed. She has never done anything. In fact, the closest she has come to physical relations is having a boy shoved against her by his friends in the school canteen, and they do this to everyone. She just happened to be standing in the queue behind them and happened to be wearing a skirt. The thing is, Althea is incredibly unattractive. Her hair is mousy and frizzy. There is a pimple on her chin and two on her forehead. Her nose is too long. All of these things – combined with the fact that her mother has brought her up to be weird, and that she is in the school orchestra – have sealed her fate forever. She will never have sex.

Althea looks at her books lined up on their shelf. Usually, she takes great comfort in books. But this evening she is simply reminded, head sideways on her tucked-up knees, that she uses them as an escape. The further her sister forays into the real world – the world of love bites, cigarettes and cheap vodka – the further Althea retreats into her own skin. In the hours she takes to fall asleep each night, Althea will fight something inside, give in and touch herself. She knows the shape of her breasts, the feel of the smooth skin on the insides of her thighs. Her fingertips know the textures inside her. She inserts several fingers, pushes soft at first, then harder and faster, until she comes against her wrist. It helps with insomnia. In the mornings she is always regretful. No one has ever told her it shouldn't be done. She is not sure if her mother even knows that a girl can do this. She just feels, somehow, that it must be wrong. Otherwise why would 'wanker' be a rude word? After the spasms of orgasm comes the thud in the chest of remembering you are alone. You are meant to have sex with men. It's meant to be them who do this to you.

It isn't just that she's never done anything, it's that whenever a rare opportunity presents itself, her mother and grandmother quickly and effectively block her, like moral ninjas. Earlier that year, Phoebe asked their mother if she could go to Life music festival. 'It's Christian, Mum,' she explained. 'All the bands sing songs about Jesus. There's no drugs or anything.'

'Do you think I should let her go?' Rosemary asked Althea.

'I don't know,' Althea said. Secretly, she hoped their mother would say no. It wasn't fair, Phoebe going off having fun while she was stuck at home.

'Will you go with her?'

'I guess so.'

While she packed her bag, she imagined herself drinking booze in a tent, which was what everyone at school said happened at Life festival. She imagined herself slipping her hand down a boy's shorts. She imagined herself going back to school with the plastic entry band around her wrist, wearing it until all the colour wore off in the shower.

She was bringing her bag to the door to put it beside Phoebe's, when Rosemary walked in and said, 'You're not going.'

'What?' Phoebe wailed. 'Mum, that's not fair. We bought the tickets!'

'I'll ask for a refund.' Rosemary sighed. 'I just can't let you go. Two girls alone on the bus. You'd have to transfer to a taxi or something at the other end. Who knows what could happen.'

And that was that.

There is the sound of shoes scuffing on the mat. The door swings open and Althea hears her sister's voice, bright as usual. 'I'm sorry, Mum, I just read your message. I didn't see it before because I was in the middle of something.'

Althea hears Rosemary stalk into the hallway. This conversation is probably going to be entertaining. She pushes her door slightly ajar.

'What exactly were you in the middle of?'

Althea, alone on her carpet, starts to grin.

'Walking to the park.'

'To meet that boy.'

'Jayden. Yes.'

'Well, you didn't tell me you were going to do that, did you?'

'Aw, Mum, I only organised to go there today. I was going to text you, but I forgot.'

'Phoebe. You are fourteen years old, and you do not go anywhere after school without your mother's knowledge. Do you understand me?'

'Yes.'

There is a silence. Althea feels the blood vessels pulsing in her cheeks.

Then Rosemary asks, 'Where else did you go?'

'Oh, nowhere, Mum. I just went to the park.'

'I don't believe you.'

'It's true, Mum! I only went to the park!'

'And what did you do in the park?'

Althea pictures the fort in the children's playground, strewn with bottles in the weekend, covered in obscene graffiti.

'Nothing much. Jayden just showed me his turtle.'

Turtle, thinks Althea, turtle. A long wrinkled neck, protruding. She can't help herself. She bursts into the hall, hair flying. 'Turtle, huh? So that's what they call it,' she shouts.

Phoebe looks at her, surprised, hurt. You are supposed to take my side, the look says. You are my sister. But Althea can't be her sister, not right now.

'What are you talking about, Althea?' Phoebe asks. There is a softer tone she uses for her older sibling.

'Althea,' says Rosemary, 'please go and take the casserole out of the oven.'

Althea walks to the kitchen. As she bends down to open the oven door, her hair falls over her eyes, and tears blur them.

'You are grounded,' says Rosemary. 'For three weeks.'

'Three weeks!' There is the sound of a schoolbag hitting the wall. 'Mum, that's not fair. I didn't even do anything!'

Althea overhears a muttered obscenity.

'Go to your room.'

'I want a glass of milk.'

'Go to your room.'

Althea is standing in the kitchen, an afghan in her hand, when Phoebe walks in. Phoebe says nothing, but gives her sister another look, this time decidedly wounded. 'It's so unfair,' Phoebe snaps, slamming the fridge door.

Althea does not reply. She picks the walnut off her biscuit and eats it with a small smile.

Billy the Pirate Poet

Nowadays I live in an ordinary house. By that I mean a 1960s three-bedder in a quiet-ish street, at a distance from the CBD that we used to call the wop-wops. I have grown out of wanting to paint enormous flowers on the walls. I notice things like the bench going rotten around the stainless-steel sink inset. I buy shoes at Kmart. People on the dole no longer come to visit and guzzle whole cartons of soy milk. I have a small daughter and in my belly a son. No one ever sleeps on the couch.

When you and I lived together, the couch was continually occupied. There being seven of us in the flat, and most of us affecting some kind of middle-class free-thinking persona, we were always taking in strays (often other middle-class free thinkers). We'd get up in the morning to get ready for work or university or a solitary bike ride, and find some tousle-haired thing stirring amidst the crochet blankets, smell a mix of stale patchouli and human body. Sometimes we'd fumble in the piles of dirty dishes, find a tea-stained mug, make whoever it was a cup of rooibos or peppermint. Other times we wouldn't bother.

It was an all-girl flat, and male couch-surfers were slightly less frequent than female ones. People used to ask us, 'But how can you stand living with so many women?' We'd shrug and tell them it was fine. Now I remember it, possibly inaccurately, as one of the happiest times of my life. I guess people were imagining a coven of harpies screeching about how much they hated men, or a bunch of eternal singletons snotting into tissues by the phone. Or a mad sect of feminists who painted murals of giant vulvas and posted sanitary pads to their enemies. I guess there was an element of truth in all of these imaginings. Now, in any case, when my mothers' group sit and chat about brands of dishwashing liquid, or compete over whose pregnancy weight gain was the lowest and who lost it the fastest, I have to keep reminding myself that you and I were not the norm. We were free thinkers, after all.

You used to write 'Artist' in the occupation box on airline forms or electoral enrolments. You embroidered over the holes in your tights; you made decorative birds with the silver card from the insides of soy milk cartons. The night Billy the Pirate Poet arrived, you were painting tiny things onto scraps of wood you'd pulled out of a dumpster a few doors down. We heard the thrum of a motorbike engine. 'That must be Joe's friend,' I said. Joe was a flatmate's brother who had recently moved to London and kept inviting people to stay with us any time they were in New Zealand. Billy had a thundering knock. When I answered the door, I saw he was a big man. Those of us who were into men tended to bring home the stringy, anaemic types whose selling point was their two-tone shoes or their spectacular glasses frames. They played the guitar and put flowers in their buttonholes, they fell hopelessly in love, they were great to go op-shopping with. One can see why so many girls went stupid over Billy. The sight of defined muscles had a hormonal effect.

Billy entered in black motorbike leathers. 'Does he have to go round in the skins of ten cows?' you muttered, swirling your paintbrush in a jar of turps. I was aroused in spite of myself. I've always had a fetish for the disapproved of, the forbidden. Sometimes I'd just about wet myself passing a handsome cop on the street, while you or whichever other of my friends hissed 'Pig' in my ear.

Billy asserted his presence by throwing his pack onto the couch, and his maleness by slouching in a chair with his legs wide apart. You had become so incensed by this point that you refused to talk. Your nose and cheeks were bright pink. It was up to me and Grace to offer Billy peppermint tea and make conversation.

'This probably sounds really weird,' said Billy. 'I mean, you probably don't do this here, but I really feel like a strong espresso.'

'No problemo,' said Grace. She was a barista, and exclusively lesbian.

'I've been travelling in Italy recently,' Billy said. 'They drink espresso any time of day or night. You only drink coffee with milk for breakfast. They think you're a right twat if you order a latte at four o'clock.'

'Wellington has the highest number of cafés per capita in the world,' you spat. This was possibly true then, before the recession hit and half of them went under.

'You'll have to show me around,' Billy said, looking at you intently. 'Take me to the best ones.' His slow smile reminded me of a worm burrowing into an apple. He had already settled on what he was going to do with you. I have always been blessed, or cursed, with the ability to see straight through people. You, on the other hand, are an aesthete. You see surfaces; you take things at face value. I often think you've had more fun than me.

By the time you went to bed, your blush had settled down and you were beginning to unclench. Billy stood behind you and went into controlled raptures over your art. He confessed his own lack of ability with a paintbrush. He professed to being good with his hands, in general. He said his main passion, however, was for writing poetry. As you walked up the stairs, he said, 'Sweet dreams.' I recall he winked at me, so quickly I wouldn't have been able to pin it on him.

In the morning you appeared in a sundress, although it was only October, and ate your Bircher muesli in a perky manner. I saddled my bicycle and headed off to work just as Billy was transferring from the couch to the kitchen table. He had thrown on a singlet and a pair of floaty Vietnamese pants, but no undies to speak of.

I spent the morning doing mundane things: sweeping up broken glass and wiping tables, emptying ashtrays, filling handles for the type of people who have their first beer at morning tea. I didn't witness what went on between you and Billy, but I imagine you did some more painting, conscious of every brush stroke, and he did some more admiring. He played you some of his awful free-jazz recordings; you applauded their mayhem and lack of resolution. He made you his version of a real Italian espresso. You found some vegan chocolate at the back of the pantry and placed two squares on each of your saucers. He spent some time writing a postcard to another girl, somewhere in England, about the beauty of the whales at Kaikōura, and the thrill of playing pool with mulleted locals. He made much of requiring a stamp. He suggested you take a walk to the shops. He turned it into an invitation to picnic in the town belt. When I arrived home at 3pm, Billy was in the bathroom shaving, and you were fizzing around the kitchen throwing cutlery and a tablecloth into a basket, and saying, 'I just feel like anything could happen.'

'Anything could,' I cautioned you. The pair of you headed out to the local New World, you with your grandmother's vintage cardigan over your sundress, the basket slung over one shoulder, and Billy in a pair of cut-off jeans and an Australian felt hat that emphasised his jawline.

That night the couch remained vacant. Those of us with rooms backing onto yours were shaken from our dreams at around midnight by a crescendo of thumping. At first I thought it was the neighbours' techno. Then I thought someone might be breaking in, not that we had anything worth stealing. It should have been obvious even before I heard the yelping and the roaring. The paintings on my wall began to jump on their hooks. An empty glass fell off my bedside table and landed on the carpet. I put my pillow over my head.

Billy stayed at our house for another fortnight or so. You sang and baked things: crumbles, ginger crunch. I invested in a pair of earplugs. Some of the flatmates grumbled about toilet seats left up, a male smell on the lino. But overall, Billy was careful to please. He stole some bread crates and constructed a two-bin compost system in our sad square of garden, lashing the crates together with inner-tube rubber. Our landlord would have flipped if he had seen the solar panel Billy made out of scavenged junk. Fortunately he never had quite the right part to connect it to the hot water cylinder. Billy was not a natural craftsman. He didn't have the patience for fiddly work like plumbing. He would have made a good cowboy, I thought. He had the same kind of testicle-dangling swagger as someone who spent a lot of time on horseback. But you had settled on his being a pirate. In your head, his many travels had been undertaken not by plane, but in a big oaken eighteenth-century ship. He was tanned and swashbuckling. Billy called you a fairy, spelled 'faerie'. You wore more pink than usual, and glittery makeup. One night before a party I found you duct-taping your breasts in a sudden fixation with cleavage. I was surprised by how depressed this made me.

In those days I was something of a closet poet. I had a few old exercise books and diaries, bought quarter-price in July, in which I would pen my creations and paste found pieces of paper, like other people's grocery receipts or cryptic letters written by paranoid schizophrenics, hand-delivered to every mailbox in Newtown. Often, or mostly, the stuff I wrote was awful. When I was stoned, especially so. I used to attend an open mic night every second Thursday at one of the local pubs. One evening I was shoving things in my dowdy backpack when Billy asked if he could tag along. You slotted your arm through his, and we made our way through the darkening streets, passing derelicts who smelled of meths and unwashed pants, students with their eyes fixed on their shoes, African mothers in head-to-toe rainbows. The pub was relatively quiet, and the patrons were mostly known to us. There was Serious Will – was he really getting himself in the mood by composing something on a sugar packet? There was Far Too Old Dave, thus named because he was the wrong side of thirty and still flatting with university kids. (I laugh about this now that I am older than Far Too Old Dave was then.) There was Jackson the bicycle mechanic, who had nursed a light flirtation with you into a wounding passion, the way a child scratches a mosquito bite and picks the subsequent scab until a fleshy scar forms. He looked deeply morose to see you at Billy's side, your head nestled into his armpit. There was Jenny Heming, a buxom New Age type who worked at the Nepalese restaurant down the road. She got talking to Billy like he was an old friend. He admired her amber beads and stared at her breasts. You kicked your shoe against a bar stool and talked louder than usual. Billy was probably skint, but bought us all a cider. This was part of his schtick – a madcap affability, a reckless generosity.

When it was my turn, I read a confessional prose poem. It featured me in the bath. The paper trembled in my hands. There was the usual tired clapping, and you let out an ululation, which I felt was gratuitous. Far Too Old Dave gave me a seedy smile. I gave him a vicious glare.

Billy read next. His work was clichéd, even by my standards. He'd written a rambling ballad of the road entitled 'Southern Country', with a few rhyming lines thrown in here and there for the ease of it. The only line I remembered was 'black as the ace of spades', which I felt was taking things too far. Serious Will bruised his sugar packet and muttered, 'Should have called it "Country Without The O".' I don't know what you thought, but you ululated some more. Out of politeness we each bought Billy a beer and shared another between ourselves. The bar owner must have eventually cottoned on to the brokeness of wannabe poets, because she canned the open mic nights shortly afterwards. You and I used to fill water bottles with vodka and tonic, smuggle them into gigs under our dresses. Or we'd drink cheap plonk at home first, smoke a spliff and then weave into town arm in arm. I remember us downing a bladder of nameless wine while waiting for the bus, drinking straight from the plastic tap, laughing so hard it ran down our faces.

Billy got talking to Jackson about bikes. The conversation quickly became boring, and after unsuccessfully sighing and rolling your eyes, you walked home with me. 'I'll see you soon,' Billy called to us, although it would be 2am before we heard the front door click.

As we turned into our street, you squeezed my arm and said, 'I think I'm in love with him.'

'Be careful,' I told you.

'And I think he really likes me,' you went on, oblivious. I couldn't talk you out of it. You were dreaming of following

Billy around the world. You were wondering if one could buy motorcycle leathers that were vegan.

Although the house prices have gone up, and some of the places that used to look semi-derelict have been painted in fashionable colours, Newtown is still much the same. The same green grocers that sell mangoes and plantain bananas, the same Indian restaurants, the same op shops. The fish 'n' chip place, the cheap bakeries. The Syrian shop with its bottles of rosewater and jars of tea. The place that sells old ladies' nightgowns. Outpatients dawdling the streets during the day, muttering to themselves. I don't often go there, nowadays. Once our playgroup went on a trip to the zoo, caught the train and bus together. Small children seem to love anything that moves. Put a kid in a carriage with seats, with a window she can press her fingers to, with the world rushing past, and she'll be happy. One of the other mums said something about how scungy it was, and another said she'd had food poisoning from the fish 'n' chips.

'I lived here for five years,' I said, mostly to myself. One of the playgroup kids was singing 'The Wheels on the Bus' and it was hard to talk over him. I shouldn't judge. I knew all the words to that song. *The mummies on the bus go blah blah blah . . .*

The Banksy-esque stencils that seemed to replicate themselves, the layers of posters for punk gigs. The punk rockers must have been in their fifties by now, knees wrecked from pogoing. There was a group of kids walking up Rintoul Street, dreadlocked and pierced, all in black. They looked like people we'd known, in younger incarnations. They'd be going home to eat lentil dal and plot the revolution.

It's maybe a forty-five-minute drive to Newtown from where I live now. In fact, my daughter was born there, in the hospital you and I used to walk or cycle past on a daily basis. I remember when they were dismantling one of the old wings, and you could see into the exposed rooms as if they'd been sliced in half. 'I don't like to look at it,' you told me. 'There are ghosts in there.' On one side of the complex there was a chimney that always steamed, and I assumed it was the laundry, but you said, 'That's where they cook up all the old body parts. You can smell it.' After that, though I'm sure it was just water vapour, I always could. Old tonsils, amputated limbs – who knows what. 'They have to cook them up somewhere,' you told me.

When Bella was born we had a corner of a room in the post-natal ward, somewhere halfway up one of those towers. But from the inside, when I looked out, I had no idea where I was. Around me, babies screamed, doors banged, the buzzers sounded constantly. I was surrounded by people and noise. A lactation consultant pulled my breasts out of my smock with scarcely a preliminary explanation. Bella fed, my nipples turned raw, and I felt as alone as I have ever felt. Only a few rooms away, life was coming forth into the world on a regular basis: bloody, pushed between legs or pulled out with giant spoons or sliced from an abdomen, held up by a masked surgeon. Everything was tubes and bags of saline and things with lights and numbers. The times Mike wasn't with me I looked out the window or at the ceiling, and I might have been on the moon. How did they keep the sheets so white, with everything that happened on them? I went through acres of maternity pads. I thought about the laundry, and what you'd said about body parts. I wondered where you were. You had a husband and kids, but I didn't know their names. You lived in the Bay of Plenty somewhere, where your husband was from. He was a roofer – good with his hands, in general. I couldn't remember which town.

*

When my final exam time came, I spent my days in the upper floors of the university library, gazing out over the seething harbour, getting side-tracked by books on ethnobotany or ancient religions. You and a group of friends were putting together an art show. We hardly saw each other, and the only trace of Billy was the occasional slick of beard shavings circling the basin. Then, after deciding to stay in town a bit longer, Billy moved into a temporarily empty room at Jackson's place. He said something to Grace about getting out of our hair, but I suspected that things were becoming a little too domestic for him. He was getting pimples from all the vegan caramel slice.

One afternoon I gave up on my books and wandered down towards the harbour. It took me a long time to get there, because I kept running into people I knew. It was often like that – there were certain streets that seemed to be populated by familiar characters. It was as if they were always there, extras sifting around a film set through which I, the protagonist, strolled pensively. Near the bucket fountain I recognised Jenny Heming. Her feral dog was stretched to the end of his lead, bathing in the water. There was a man with her too, his hand on the small of her back. His long hair was loose, his boots familiar. Before he could avoid my eye, Jenny was waving and calling out her usual gregarious greeting. No one could really be that happy to see me. Around the hem of Jenny's skirt, tiny bells jingled. Her feet were bare apart from a toe ring. She grabbed Billy's arm. 'Amy, you know Billy, don't you.'

'Yes,' I said, smiling politely at him. It was the first time I'd seen his face betray discomfort. He actually looked shifty. 'Billy was staying at our place for a while,' I reminded her. I knew he was counting on my cooperation, and I decided I would allow it for the time being. Perhaps this was my first act of disloyalty. But as I told myself then, I didn't even really know if he was still sleeping with you. And in any case, perhaps he'd explained to you that it wasn't an exclusive arrangement.

Jenny was babbling. I watched Billy's face as she described her trip to Nelson and Golden Bay, all the beautiful people she had met and all the yummy organic wholefood she had eaten and the yoga she had done. 'And then I saw Billy getting off the Interislander, and I was like, Whoa, hi! I just felt like we were both there for a reason.' Billy's reasons, I suspected, were slightly less cosmic than hers. 'And you know what else is really funny,' Jenny went on. 'Billy is from Manchester, and I lived in Manchester for six months!'

'A fine coincidence,' Billy volunteered.

Jenny wrinkled her nose at him then turned back to me. 'Oh, I don't believe in coincidence,' she said. 'Nothing is ever a coincidence. I believe in fate.'

After my last exam I left the campus alone, feeling deflated. So that was it. University was over. If I passed everything, I would have a BA with a double major in English and anthropology. What would that make me? Unemployed, I thought. I would just have to keep working at the pub. Maybe if I really slaved at it, and drank less, I could save for a ticket to Europe. There, I would probably wind up in London, working in another pub, maybe earning more, but spending more on the same amount of booze. Life was seeming pretty pointless by the time I got home. Everyone was out. I stood outside your bedroom door and stared in. Your bed was a big unmade mess. Your floor was strewn with dresses you'd tried on and decided against. In one corner was a pair of pink lacy cheekies. I'm not sure why that embarrassed me. There were condoms strewn across your dresser, among the necklaces and cosmetics. I wondered if you had a few guys on the go. I hoped you did.

I decided to go for a bike ride. Pedalling into the southerly ought to blow out the cobwebs. I was not happy with the clanking of the chain as I jumped off the footpath onto the road. The brakes felt sloppy. I decided I would stop by Jackson's bike workshop on the way out to the south coast.

Jackson was his usual discourteous self. I began to see why he hadn't got anywhere with you. Or any other girl. He was broke. The weather was terrible. The government were evil. I felt jubilant in comparison. I asked him about his house and then, out of curiosity, about how Billy was fitting in. I didn't need to pry further – it all came out. He was a wanker. He was an arsehole. Jenny Heming was staying over on a regular basis, but it wasn't just her. Did I know he'd had three different girls there, in the last week alone?

'That's a good effort,' I joked.

'Huh,' said Jackson. 'Wasn't he seeing Bridget?'

'As far as I know, he might still be,' I said. 'I haven't seen either of them lately. I thought she might have been round at your place.'

'You should really tell her what's going on.'

I suggested that he could. He didn't think so, and anyway I was your best mate.

'Maybe she knows.' I shrugged. 'Maybe she doesn't care. She could be seeing lots of guys too.' Jackson had worked himself into an even worse state of despair. If I didn't change the topic, he would wreck my bike. I'd got as far as asking him what he was doing over summer, when the door was flung open and Billy walked in.

Billy and I greeted each other, Billy gave Jackson's back a matey slap, Jackson grunted. After the requisite enquiries after our health, Billy asked Jackson whether he was busy right now, and whether he'd be able to do him a small favour.

'Actually, I *am* busy,' said Jackson, torturing an adjustable wrench. 'I'm working on Amy's bike right now, not to mention half a million other fucking bikes.'

I felt a stab of guilt. 'It isn't really urgent. I can bring it in another time.'

'No, it's fine, I'll do it. I just don't have time to run round doing people favours, that's all.'

Billy looked out the window and whistled softly. Then he regarded me with a smile.

'What was it you needed help with?' I asked.

'Depends how strong you are.'

I rolled up a sleeve and showed him a bicep. Big arm muscles run in my maternal line. That and menopausal beards. I always tell people it's something to look forward to.

'I bought a bed at the Salvation Army,' Billy explained. 'It's not a long walk from there to the flat. If I had another pair of hands, we could carry it.'

'Is it guaranteed free of bedbugs?' asked Jackson. He was a believer in the yogic art of sleeping on a camping roll. Everyone I knew had a second-hand bed. Mine was found on the side of the road. It was mostly free of stains, and only had one spring poking through, which could be avoided in most sleeping angles.

'No problem,' I said to Billy. And to Jackson, 'No rush with the bike, I can come back whenever.'

I imagined we'd take half an hour, but when I saw the bed in the window with a 'Sold' sticker on it, I realised it would be much longer.

'It was so cheap,' said Billy. 'I'm sure it's not as heavy as it looks.'

It was a four-poster. The posts were turned wood, spray painted gold, full of borer. On the headboard was a plasterwork Cupid with a third of his face smashed off. It had no canopy, but Billy reckoned he had some Indian fabric that would do the job. We'd take the bed first and then come back for the mattress.

I began to regret my muscle display as we were exiting the shop. People passing on the street laughed at us. Someone made a lewd suggestion. I turned scarlet from the effort and the embarrassment. None of it seemed to faze Billy.

'There,' said Billy, as we finally lowered the mattress into place. It was floppy and had that op-shop aroma of feet and stale lavender perfume. I helped him tie a piece of patterned muslin onto the posts. Then, although it was starting to feel overly intimate, we found some communal sheets in the hot water cupboard and made the bed up. We hung someone's embroidered tablecloth over the Cupid. 'He's creepy,' we agreed.

'Now,' said Billy, 'I just need to know if it's all right with two people on it.' I lay next to him. 'I got a new tattoo on the weekend,' he said, and took off his shirt. It was an appropriated Māori pattern around his upper arm. 'I went up to Taupō to go skydiving, and I thought, I want to mark this occasion with some ink.'

'You have a lot of tattoos.' I thought it would be polite to remove an item of my own clothing, but I wasn't sure what. He had a couple of swallows on his chest, some Chinese characters on his belly. Down his spine swooped a dragon, the kind that breathes fire and eats princesses. The pirate fantasy must have been sparked by the anchor on his bicep.

'That was my first,' he said. 'I went into the shop and said, "What's the cheesiest thing I can get?"'

'It'd be that or a heart with your mother's name.'

'Yeah, and we don't get on, unfortunately.' We were both lying on our backs. He humped the air a few times, made the mattress buck. 'What do you reckon – it pass the test?'

'I guess so,' I said. 'It would depend how much exercise you gave it.'

'Good.' Billy sat up. I asked him to tell me some more about skydiving, which he did, and then, in a way that made it seem purely accidental, he reached for his cigarettes on the bedside table, fell on me, and did he kiss me, or did I kiss him? I recall he tasted of Port Royal tobacco, his skin smelled of tea tree. For a man purportedly so good with his hands, he was surprisingly imprecise. The sky began to darken. Birds were sounding out their roosting calls. Billy moved like a battering ram.

After what seemed like hours, and probably was, he leaned on his elbow and said, 'Erm, do you think you might come soon?'

I laughed. I felt bruised. 'No,' I admitted.

'Neither.' Billy rolled onto his stomach. 'Do you mind if I stop, then?'

'Not at all.' Perhaps I would cry.

'It's not your fault,' he said. 'It's the pills.' I must have frowned. 'Antidepressants, nothing exciting,' he explained. 'If I don't take 'em I just can't even get up in the morning. But it takes me about three days to reach orgasm.'

'Oh.' Everything was starting to fit together.

'Yeah, I have severe depression. It's why I can't keep a steady job. I just do odd stuff until I've saved enough money to go to . . . well, you know, wherever the dart falls on the map, so to speak.'

'You need to sell some poems.' For the first time, but not the last, I felt genuinely sorry for Billy.

*

I work in my garden, and when I look up, I see trains travelling the line of hills on the other side of the valley. I watch the colours of the containers, the patterns of bombing on their sides. Do you remember our street-art phase? We did stencils around town, modified billboards and ads in bus shelters. We drew armpit hair on the models in ice cream ads, pasted up speech bubbles with things like 'Capitalism is killing my soul' or 'Get me outta this plastic nightmare'. One night we decided we'd go to the train yard. You'd practised spray-painting a voluptuous naked woman with flowing hair and colourful pubes. 'I just want to see more hairy pussies in the public arena,' you told me, dead serious. She was going to be your signature character. You'd put her on containers, warehouses, empty billboards. We walked up to the fence in our weird clothes like a two-woman circus, backpacks rattling. You thought you saw a security guard and made me hide with you behind a shed. Eventually we decided to just do the back of the shed. Sometimes, afterwards, from the motorway, I'd catch a glimpse of pink painted flesh. I wonder if she is still there.

Bella is wearing waterproof overalls, digging in the soil I have just bared. Even feijoas struggle to crop in this cold climate, on these windy hills. There are not enough sunlight hours for pumpkins. I can get silverbeet to grow, and broccoli. Bella picks off the shoots and eats them. Sometimes she eats bugs, pulls worms in half. It is just us, out here, and the line of cars passing, and the occasional train. My back is sore, and my belly is huge. I step into the spade, pushing it down, and wonder if I'm tearing things up, deep inside. If gardening while pregnant might make your vagina turn inside out a few decades on. Take you by surprise in the library or the supermarket aisle. You're reading a blurb or the ingredients on a packet of biscuits and *pop!* there it goes.

The second-last time I saw you was about five years ago. You'd been living in Melbourne, and we'd stayed in touch on and off. The odd email, the odd hand-written letter. We met up for coffee, hugged half-heartedly. Our conversation never strayed into the intimate. It was just like a conversation at work: banal, without risk. Living somewhere bigger and hotter had shaped and coloured you differently. Your hair was a few shades lighter, your skin tanned. You were louder, brighter. Brassy. You were working in a graphic design agency. You painted only for home-décor purposes. Sculpture took up too much space, you'd given that away. I had shelved the idea of being a poet. I owned more than two pairs of shoes, wore colour-coordinated clothes and no longer believed that human hair was self-cleaning. I got up early, stayed up late, slept with a lot of men, and drank a lot. I was working in communications and going to lots of BYO dinners with 'the girls', who weren't really the girls, not in the way you and I and our other close friends had been. Do you remember we used to lie cuddled up on the couch together? One of us spooning the other, the crochet blanket over us, the cushions smelling of spilt tea. One of our flatmates said when she moved in she'd assumed we were a couple. My mum was always quizzing me about who in the flat was lesbian and who was bi and who was straight, or straight-ish. I told her we had a wheel that we spun and each day it was decided who'd be what. At the time I thought Mum was just being voyeuristic, but now I think she wanted to know if I was in love with you. Bridget, I wasn't. We were friends, but we were also soulmates. It still seems weird to me that we could have fallen out over such a tosser. Such a two-dimensional drongo. A pirate poet! A broke guy with as many STIs as a medical textbook. Maybe it wasn't just that. Maybe we were always going to go our separate ways. Not growing up – I've never felt like that has happened – but growing out and away from each other, and away from that age of grand dreams. Someday I looked in the mirror and saw lines forming around my eyes, the beginnings of grey, and knew that possibilities had narrowed themselves, that I wouldn't live forever.

Sometimes I feel like I'll die out here. Not that I'll live here until I'm old, but that I'll just waste away, or die of boredom. Someone will find me lying among the rows of broccoli, wind ruffling my hair, Bella poking around me with her small fork.

It was the opening night of your group art show. You were very excited. You wore high heels and a hat with a feather in it, a close-fitting black dress with a plunging neckline. You'd probably taped your tits again. We both wore makeup and, in that way peculiar to women who seldom do, we both looked like drag queens. My one pair of presentable shoes had got wet in the rain, so I was wearing my hiking boots.

I hugged you. I remember that hug, the firm squeeze of it. We hung out together by the drinks table, sipping cask wine out of paper cups. You kept peeping over my shoulder; it was obvious you were scanning the door. Lots of people we knew were there: our flatties, Jackson, Serious Will. And Far Too Old Dave, defying gravity as usual.

'I wonder where Billy is,' you said.

'I dunno,' I said. 'You could ask Jackson.'

'What would he know?' You tossed your head, the feather fluttered. I really hoped he wouldn't show up, and to my relief, and your consternation, he didn't. It was nearly speech time, everyone was tipsy and you were nail-biting. 'Where is he?' you said.

'Bridget, he's not worth making a fuss over.'

'But he's a pirate. And he's a poet.'

'Sounds like a jerk to me,' said your co-artist Laney, who had overheard us.

'I just don't get him,' you confessed. 'I mean, he's sort of all hot and cold. Sometimes he wants to see me, other times he goes away for days, says he's going skydiving, and stuff. I said I'd go with him, if I could afford it, but of course I can't.'

'Maybe you're not the only chippy in the packet,' said Laney.

'Oh.' You laughed. 'He would have told me.'

So, in my blundering way, I told you about Jenny Heming, about the other girls Jackson had described. I chickened out of telling you about me, but you said, 'I suppose you fucked him too,' and when I bent down to re-lace my boot, you flew into a rage.

'Well, neither of us came, so it didn't really count,' I said. But you stormed off, saying to Laney, 'You do the speech. I can't. Amy's been fucking my boyfriend.'

I walked outside to join the smokers. I was blinking back tears. 'Been fucking' was an exaggeration: it was only once, and as I said, no one came. And so was 'boyfriend', for that matter. Someone who's sharing their crabs with half of Wellington doesn't merit that term. I had never smoked, but I bummed a rollie off Far Too Old Dave and stood there puffing indignantly, throwing in my two cents' worth on whatever people were talking about. To hell with convention. I could even screw Dave if I felt like it. From now on, anything.

You must have got drunk. You didn't surface from your room the next day. I knocked at 3pm but there was no answer. I knocked again at four and heard you moan an obscene request for me to leave, including where I could go and what act I could perform upon myself. I walked in anyway. 'Are you OK?' I asked.

You said that whatever your condition, it was unlikely I cared.

'Don't be stupid,' I said. 'You're my best friend.'

'Well, you haven't behaved like it.'

'Bridget, I can't believe you are getting so upset about such a loser. He's a male slut. He's not worth following to Lower Hutt, let alone the other side of the world. And,' I added, 'do you know he's mentally unwell?'

'He is not,' you said. 'You're making that up.'

'He told me,' I said. 'He's been on antidepressants for five years. That's why he can't, you know . . .'

You sat up. Your face was swollen. You yelled all the traditional things at me, insinuating that I was illegitimate, given to incestuous activities and providing sexual services for remuneration, and suffering from various fungal and bacterial diseases. 'I am moving out,' you screamed in my face. 'So stick that up your stupid arse!'

'I'll move out,' I offered, gallantly. 'I'll go and stay with my sister for a while.' I was good about it, I felt. I paid my two weeks' notice, even though I was gone that evening. I didn't have much stuff to pack up.

I saw you in town the other day. Although we have never looked alike, in some ways it was like looking at my own reflection. The same feeling of shock at the gathering skin around the jaw, the descended bosom, the thickened upper arms. 'Amy,' you called across Cuba Mall. You looked at my rounded bulk. 'Oh my god! You're pregnant!' I couldn't sense any real excitement in your voice.

'Yeah,' I said, and pointed towards the bucket fountain. 'And that's Bella. She'll be two in a couple of weeks.'

'My kids are at their grandparents' for the weekend,' you told me. 'Me and Josh are down here for adult time. He's going to the rugby and I'm having some retail therapy.'

'Oh, well,' I said. 'Come out for a cuppa if you get bored of that.'

'Yeah, maybe.' I suspected you wouldn't. 'Bella,' you called. 'Bella!' She turned around, face sticky, hands dripping. You held out your arms. 'Say hello to Aunty Bridge.' Bella started to climb into the fountain. I remembered Jenny Heming's dog. I pulled her out, held her awkwardly on my hip, against my belly. 'She looks just like you,' you said.

'Thanks. Everyone else says she looks like Mike's mother.'

We chatted for a while – there is no other word for it, that inane and soulless way of talking. We exchanged numbers. Your phone looked expensive and your clothes weren't handmade or even second-hand. As you gave me a limp hug and walked away, I looked around me and realised that apart from you, I didn't recognise anyone on the street.

A summer of scents

It was a summer of scents. First, the sweet, cabbagey smell of canola flowers, high and yellow in the fields. Asparagus stallholders set up at their regular stops and everyone's kitchens filled with the aroma of the steaming white spears. People moved outside onto their patios, lawns and allotments; kids kicked balls; meat and sausages were grilled. In the fruit grocer's the first strawberries arrived, crushed and reeking of sunshine.

By the middle of June, the daily average temperature had reached the late thirties. Frau Dickmann did not like the heat. It made her ankles swell and her face puff and blotch. No amount of makeup hid the redness; no powder could hold her sweats. When she opened the doors onto the balcony in the mornings, the air felt like the hot breath of a dog, slavering in her face. It was oppressive. The sound of skylarks singing did not cheer her. Farm vehicles passed and filled her lounge with odours of manure and diesel. Her only comforts were the TV, visits from her friends and outings to the department store or supermarket. There the air was conditioned, cooled. It smelled only of new clothes and lettuce.

On the morning of the fourteenth of June, Frau Dickmann rose wet and afraid. She had slept under a sheet and a blanket, having felt cold around 2am. Now she was soaked in sweat and had been having intense nightmares about her husband, deceased for three years. She went to the bathroom and coughed into the sink. There was a greenish colour and a small trace of blood. She ran herself a cold bath and lay there for a quarter hour. Then she plucked her eyebrows to a wavering line a hair thick, put firming cream on her face, drew over the line with a dark brown pencil. Her hair was bright red with white at the roots. She put some curlers in and went to get dressed.

Next door, Frau Müller was clothed in Lycra and doing step aerobics to a video she had bought twenty years before. It had sat on a shelf unused for most of that time, but this summer the sight of her own body nude while bathing at the lakes had been enough to spur Frau Müller into an exercise regime. At around 8am, the sun's brilliance broke through the privacy curtains, and she switched off the TV and VCR, drank two glasses of banana juice and went downstairs to the garage to find her bicycle. Frau Müller was going to pick berry fruit at her allotment. It was important to get them before the sun was on them too long.

Upstairs, Herr Rabe's apartment smelled of eggs and herring fillets. He had been to the Konsum and bought his daily bread rolls, and was now smearing them with butter and paté. He liked his eggs quite runny. When he cracked the first one with his ingenious Swiss tool, designed solely for that purpose, a trail of yolk seeped out of it. There was nothing much in the news. There had been a fight between the fans of the rival football teams, but that happened most weekends. The police were still hunting for a man who had left a girl's body in a backyard pond. The public library was going to be closed for two months in a remodelling project that would cost the council millions and involve a team of architects. Herr Rabe hated architects. This last item upset him particularly. 'In all this heat,' he grumbled. Most people's thoughts, he surmised, would be turning to a cool and quiet place where they could read books. If it hadn't been a Saturday, he would have rung the council and complained.

Frau Dickmann was making blackcurrant jam. Frau Müller, her best friend, had so many currants in the allotment that she was thinking of cutting out a bush. 'You must never do that,' said Frau Dickmann. 'We can make preserves and sell them. I read in a magazine, blackcurrants are one of the top twenty foods for fighting cancer.' This was enough to convince Frau Müller, whose husband had succumbed to cancer of the pancreas seven years back.

The blackcurrants and the sugar slowly melted together on the stove, and sweetness filled the apartment. Herr Rabe could smell it upstairs and it maddened him. It was a feeling he'd often had as a small boy: an irresistible desire for sugar biscuits.

The smell gave Frau Dickmann a headache. She chopped a raw carrot, put the pieces in a bowl and ate them in front of the TV. Every channel was worse than the last. A documentary on Napoleon. A documentary on the Stasi. An overdubbed American sitcom. An intolerable man with long hair visiting the Antarctic. Merkel mumbling her words of nothing. Frau Dickmann hated politicians, all of them. She and her husband had religiously hated the Communists. The wall had come down and they'd voted in real elections, had high hopes that were quickly dashed. Nothing much seemed to have changed for Frau Dickmann, except that her son had gone to Norway, and she was able to buy more stuff than ever before.

On her way out of the driveway, Frau Müller passed Jürgen Schulz coming home on his two-stroke scooter. It made an ear-splitting racket. Jürgen was red-eyed and unkempt, still drunk from the night before. He gave Frau Müller a wave and fell into the gate post. Frau Müller knew exactly what was wrong and didn't stop to help him. At the allotment she picked currants, strawberries and raspberries, and tucked them into her bicycle basket in margarine containers. The cherries weren't quite ripe. She surveyed the tree for bird damage. She would need some netting soon. She went to pick a cauliflower and found that all her spring onions had been flattened. She swore. Unbeknownst to her, the Kübler's boy, full of stolen vodka and beer, had professed his love to Marie Fleischer in this spot last night. He had then discovered what the place between a girl's legs really felt like, which, although pleasant, had taken him by surprise. Marie had gone home with her dress green and stinking.

Oma Kübler was weeding carrots in the garden next door, her gigantic bum in the air. Frau Müller showed her the forlorn onions. Oma Kübler frowned. 'The children were here last night,' she said. 'I don't have any spring onions, but in two weeks, I can give you plenty of garlic.' She passed her a kohlrabi for good measure, and Frau Müller reciprocated with a small bunch of radishes.

And so the morning passed. Frau Dickmann poured her jam into washed and sterilised jars, cut circles of fabric and fastened them with rubber bands around the tops. In her crooked handwriting she inscribed the date and the fruit varieties on a sheet of stickers and stuck them to the jars. Frau Dickmann had had the shakes for years. It was terrible, arthritis. If it got any worse, she'd told her daughter, she would have to hang herself.

Frau Müller appeared at her door with more blackcurrants. 'I picked them just now,' she said. 'They won't come fresher.'

*

Upstairs, Herr Rabe lay down on the settee for his afternoon nap. Although he had quit smoking ten years prior, the brown acrylic fabric still smelled like cigarettes. It was comforting. Herr Rabe did not like sleeping in his bedroom during the daytime.

He fell asleep swiftly, his whiskers twitching, mouth open, drool leaking at the lower corner. Herr Rabe had not slept well the night before. He was an early riser and liked to go early to bed, which at this time of year, near the solstice, meant before sundown. But last night, the thirteenth of June, his next-door neighbour Jürgen Schulz had woken him half an hour later with the throbbing assault of some of the worst electronic music he had ever heard.

Jürgen was something of a misfit. Although he had moved out of his parents' home and was now renting an apartment by himself, he had failed, by the age of thirty-seven, to procure himself a wife, children or a steady job, and was therefore regarded by most as an irretrievable loser. Jürgen lived for computers, drinking and sex, which, despite his receding hairline and pillowy middle, he still occasionally managed to have.

Although his music had woken Herr Rabe, and although Herr Rabe had subsequently suffered fits of insomnia between then and sunrise, Jürgen was unaware of it and would have been genuinely sorry to know he was depriving an old man of his sleep. On the night of Friday the thirteenth of June, it simply hadn't occurred to Jürgen that anyone would be trying to sleep before 10pm. As his stereo blared in the living room, Jürgen changed his clothes in the bedroom, put on the patent leather brogues that made him look like a pimp. In the bathroom he applied a sticky substance to his hair, squeezed a couple of blackheads from the side of his nose. Seeing an open magazine slumped beside the toilet, a shaven vulva presenting itself in the centrefold, he considered a quick wank but decided against it. Tonight, he might just get lucky.

In the basement garage, Jürgen mounted his yellow Schwalbe and started its puttery engine. Two-stroke exhaust filled his nose as he swung out the roller door and round to the gate. He took the back roads past a pig farm, through avenues of untended apple trees. Passing the allotments, he caught a whiff of a woman's perfume. It was in fact the scent of Marie Fleischer, who had over-applied Dior J'Adore and was walking to drink with Oskar Kübler and his siblings at their grandparents' allotment. The little bungalow had couches and a refrigerator and was, all in all, a perfect place for teenagers to hide.

Jürgen reached the carpark at the lake, where a bunch of his friends and loose associates were gathered for an outdoor party. There came the clink of beer bottles, the booming of a drunk braggart and shrieks of laughter from inebriated women. The lake smelled faintly of microscopic algae. Jürgen suddenly felt alone and very sober, although he had consumed a fair amount of his uncle's plum schnapps prior to departure.

As he was walking from the carpark to the shore, a figure materialised out of the darkness.

'God in fucking heaven,' shouted Jürgen. 'You gave me a fright!' It was his neighbour from down the hall, Martin Engel, whom he had personally invited. Martin gave his apologies but said he was developing a migraine and really must go home. Martin was prone to migraines. He must have been prone to a lot of things: he was on a sickness benefit for some reason, and seldom left his apartment. He was always incredibly polite, impeccably groomed and generally pleasant to associate with, but this evening Jürgen just shrugged his shoulders, farewelled him, expressed a hope for his swift recovery, and then thought to himself that there really wasn't any helping this man. Jürgen suspected the migraine was an excuse, and that Martin had found being in a social situation too unbearable. 'His loss,' Jürgen said to himself, and joined the throng.

Martin Engel walked away from the lake. If anyone had been watching him, they might have been alarmed by the perfectly blank expression on his face, the numb plodding of his feet. He had the disconnected appearance of an astronaut cut loose during a space-walk, floating in the void.

He walked the two and a half kilometres home along the same shortcut that Jürgen Schulz had taken on his Schwalbe. No one crossed his path, no passing cars lit his way, there were no streetlights. The first sign of life he encountered was the rasping of young breath as he passed the Kübler's allotment. His vision was blurring, but he made out two prone figures in a corner of the vegetable patch. The sharp scent of spring onions hit his nose. Between the allotment and the apartment block, he saw two cats, a scruffy old man with a scruffy white dog, a kid on a BMX and a mother walking her infant to sleep. He took the stairs, unlocked his front door and breathed in the welcome and friendly silence of his rooms.

On the seventeenth of June, Herr Rabe returned home from the doctor in a rage. His tachycardia had been playing up again, and he suspected his medication needed reviewing. Dr Fuchs, his doctor of forty-six years, was away on stress leave, so he was referred to a young woman who, her office wall proclaimed, had also completed a certificate in alternative medicine. She had long, loose blond hair and a constant smile. Herr Rabe disliked her immediately. No sooner had he mentioned the tachycardia than she started to ask him preposterous questions about diet, drinking, exercise and stress. Herr Rabe demanded that she take his blood pressure and listen to his heart like a doctor ought to. The young doctor reassured him that she would do this in good time. She made some suggestions for stress reduction, including going for leisurely walks, swimming and sex. When she mentioned the latter, Herr Rabe's fury could no longer be contained. 'Are you crazy?' he shouted. The doctor continued to sit there in her swivel chair, smiling obligingly. Herr Rabe muttered some curse words and stomped out of the room.

As he walked to the bus stop, thinking over the unpleasant incident, he was reminded of the time he and his ex-wife went to a specialist about his impending impotence. The specialist suggested he take longer over foreplay and spend time gazing at his wife's naked body. Herr Rabe looked at his wife and decided it was her fault. No one could gaze at her nakedness and maintain an erection. However, after the divorce, subsequent experiments eventually convinced him that the problem had a mechanical basis.

Now, Herr Rabe could hardly imagine having sex. It had been so many years that the only thing he felt when he thought about it was a regretful anger. His wife had ruined him, starved the passion from his life. And more to the point, who would he do it with? He walked up the steps to the apartment block's front entrance behind Frau Dickmann, who was carrying a basket of groceries. Her enormous butt was as wide as a door jamb and tapered to a pudgy crack visible through her tights. Immodest, at her age, Herr Rabe thought. Imagine getting on top of that aberration. The heaving meat, the squeaky noises emitting from the hole in the face. Like fucking a cow that has died of bloat.

*

Frau Dickmann went into her apartment and placed the basket on the kitchen bench with a heavy sigh. Phlegm was rising in her throat; her skin was awash. The walk from the shops was not far, but the sun was genuinely awful. She took the items out of the basket one by one: orange juice, milk, a cabbage, pottles of chocolate and caramel quark for when her granddaughters came to visit. A bottle of rum. Today Frau Dickmann was going to make rumtopf. Earlier that morning, Frau Müller had come around with strawberries, more currants and the first of the cherries from her allotment. She had put the bird netting up just in time. Frau Dickmann lifted the bottle to the light and placed it down again. She had a rule not to drink before midday. It was a minute to. She watched the second-hand move around the clock face, poured herself a small glass and downed it in a gulp. Ugh. It was good rum. The fruit would soak in it, in the big crystal jar that had been her mother's. As the summer wore on she would add more fruit: blackberries, apricots. Come winter, she and Frau Müller would sit in front of the TV and eat the rumtopf with vanilla ice cream and eierlikör. Frau Müller would lament her ageing shape and help herself to seconds.

Frau Dickmann put away the groceries, got out a clean chopping board, washed the fruit, cut the tops off the strawberries, stoned the cherries, slid them into the jar. Coloured juice splashed up the glass. She poured in enough rum to cover the fruit, leaned over and breathed in all the good smells. And again. On the third deep inhalation, Frau Dickmann realised there was another smell in the background, and that smell was unpleasant.

Perhaps it had been there for days. Perhaps it had grown slowly, like a lightbulb on a dimmer increasing in brightness.

She'd been aware of it, but now it was definite. Frau Dickmann sniffed again. Frau Kümmel's little cat might have brought something in. Or rats might have got into the building somehow, might be living in the ceiling cavities. The more she sniffed, the more she smelled it. It began to bother her so much that she went to knock on Frau Müller's door.

Frau Müller had noticed it too. 'I thought it was the dumpsters,' she said. 'All this heat, cooking all the food scraps and rubbish in there.' No, Frau Dickmann shook her head. It was inside the building, that was for certain. She would ask Frau Kümmel.

Frau Kümmel lived on the other side of Frau Müller. She was over ninety, bent almost in half and mostly deaf. Frau Dickmann waved her hands around and talked loudly and Frau Kümmel nodded and smiled. Frau Dickmann could see through to the living room, where Frau Kümmel's cat was licking its paws on a sunny armchair. Frau Dickmann pointed at it, suggesting that it had hidden a kill, exaggerating all the movements of her lips. 'Yes, my good pussycat,' smiled Frau Kümmel. Frau Dickmann gave up and went to get her neighbour a jar of jam instead.

By the nineteenth of June the smell was overpowering. Nothing else could be inhaled without a whiff of it: the morning coffee, the newly cut grass in the adjacent park. Even Herr Rabe, with his ex-smoker's damaged nose, could not bear it. Frau Dickmann came pounding on his door one afternoon, almost in tears.

'It must be rats,' she told him.

Herr Rabe nodded, so agitated by the smell that he forgot how much he disliked her. 'Come in,' he said. 'We'll ring the council.'

Frau Dickmann looked around Herr Rabe's apartment and pitied him. Along one side of his living room was a big wall unit from the Communist days, that generic dark wood. Its shelves were piled with magazines and ancient books. Everything in the room seemed dated and tired and brown. Under the pervasive pungent smell there was the old reek of stale cigarettes. The whole place was fusty, as though the windows were never opened, and the sun burned through the glass, frying the Formica and filling the room with antique chemicals. Frau Dickmann thought she and Frau Müller were doing just fine on their own, but Herr Rabe's apartment without a woman in it was like a deserted city or a dead landscape.

The housing department put Herr Rabe on hold, poured gut-churning pop music into his ear. He cursed audibly. Was his telephone also a relic of the DDR? Frau Dickmann could have sworn it was. She remembered life without a phone, when she'd had to go to her sister's place to make a call. Even after the wall came down, and Karsten went off to Scandinavia never to return, it took them years to get phone lines installed. Perhaps Herr Rabe had been Stasi, and had been rewarded for spying on his neighbours. 'No, that will not work,' he was shouting now. 'Monday is not acceptable! Today or tomorrow at the very latest.' He slammed the handset back into the receiver.

'I'll ring them too,' Frau Dickmann said. She would knock on all the doors and tell everyone in the building, all four floors, to do the same. Her granddaughters were supposed to come today after school, but it simply wasn't possible to immerse children in such a stink. She would have to call their mother and put them off.

Herr Rabe felt his chest tighten as Frau Dickmann headed back down the stairwell. Frau Dickmann's daughter lived locally, and she visited with her on a regular basis. Herr Rabe's son, an only child, was on the other side of the country in Aachen. He hadn't seen him in twenty years. There were no letters, no phone calls, and Herr Rabe mistrusted the internet. His son had taken his wife's side in the divorce, that was the fact of the matter. He'd be forty-two now, with a family of his own. Herr Rabe didn't know if he had grandchildren but felt that he must. He thought about his neighbour Martin Engel, about the same age as his son, who also lived alone. Come to think of it, he hadn't seen him in a while either – but that was hardly unusual. The man was a committed recluse.

On Monday the twenty-third of June, Frau Dickmann rang the authorities for the third time. She had been around the whole apartment block and spoken to everyone apart from Jürgen Schulz, Martin Engel and the Bauers on the fourth floor, who were on holiday in Tenerife. It was not good enough. The council should have sent someone right away. The woman on the phone spoke briskly. Someone would come within the next twenty-four hours to inspect the building.

Frau Dickmann and Frau Müller caught the bus into town and went to a Turkish place for lunch. Frau Müller confessed she longed to travel but didn't want to spend the money nor go alone. The smells of the restaurant – sliced cabbage, frying meat, fresh bread – were an elixir to their noses after the pong of home.

'Why don't we put aside a little bit from our pensions, and go together,' Frau Dickmann suggested. 'But you have to be careful with your money. Karsten was there with his family a few years ago. He said they'll overcharge you like crazy if you let them. You have to be prepared to haggle.'

'I would like to see the ruins,' said Frau Müller, 'and the beaches. But, you do have to wear clothes on the beach. Not like here.'

The following day, Frau Dickmann sat on her couch waiting for the building inspector. In any case, she had decided to go and stay with her daughter. She was on the phone to her now, making arrangements. Frau Dickmann's daughter, mother of three girls under five, sounded tired and peeved. 'Of course you can have Marianne's room,' she was saying. 'It's no trouble at all. She can clean up all her pencils and clothes off the floor and it's yours.' Frau Dickmann knew to go along with her, even when she was saying the opposite of what she felt. Her daughter's husband was a difficult man. But her other local relative, a sister, had only one bedroom, a husband and a dog. Dogs made Frau Dickmann wheeze. Instinctively, she looked upwards for solace, and that was when she saw the ceiling was leaking.

A thick brown liquid had pooled on the ceiling panels and was oozing through. That was where the smell was coming from. Something was leaking in there. Something had perhaps melted and seeped through from the room above. But the smell wasn't only here – it had made its way into every apartment in the building. Whatever it was must be substantial. The apartment directly above Frau Dickmann's was inhabited by Martin Engel. He was scarcely seen, came and went like a ghost, never made a noise. He was always clean and well-dressed. It was unlike him, Frau Dickmann thought, to pollute the building with something large and smelly.

The brown stain sat along the seam of wall and ceiling, adjacent to Frau Müller's. Frau Dickmann went next door and knocked. Frau Müller hit pause on the aerobics and came to the door in her leotard and tights, her armpit hair damp and spiky. Frau Dickmann pointed. Frau Müller could see it too. She fetched the step-ladder from her kitchen and reached up to poke the ceiling panels. The stain was wet and stank of the worst things imaginable.

The two women went directly upstairs without a word. But when they got to the door of Martin Engel's apartment, the building inspector was there with the police, and they were carrying out something in a long plastic bag.

On Friday the thirteenth of June, Martin Engel felt the silence of his apartment around him like a comforting blanket. He had successfully escaped the lakeside party he had only attended as a gesture of politeness. Jürgen was still out and unlikely to return any time soon. Herr Rabe was asleep – if Martin pressed his ear to the kitchen wall, he could hear him snoring softly in his bed on the other side. The man was a venomous old crank, but Martin felt a strange kind of warmth towards him in that moment.

Martin took all the perishables out of the fridge and put them into a garbage sack, wiped down the glass trays and turned off the fridge at the wall. He put a tea towel over the door to keep it from sealing shut and going mouldy inside. He emptied the bins from the kitchen and bathroom into the same sack, carried it downstairs and put it into the dumpster. He stripped his bed, washed the sheets and, when the cycle was done, put them in the dryer. He folded them and put them away in the linen closet. He swept the linoleum floors, but did not vacuum the carpet for fear of waking Herr Rabe. He put the plug in the sink and half filled it with water. He took all his pot plants and put them in the sink. He sat down at his kitchen table and swallowed a bottle of pills, one by one, as monotonous as days.

August came and the elder bushes in Frau Müller's allotment began to fruit. Frau Müller picked basketfuls, set them in a steamer to make cordial. Dark red juice ran down out of them like blood. Frau Müller added sugar and bottled it. The tiny allotment bungalow had been her temporary home for six weeks now. There was a small kitchen bench, a single bed, a couch, a fridge, an old TV. But it was hopelessly cramped. Frau Dickmann had found them new apartments in an identical Plattenbau on the other side of town. The Communists got a few things right, Frau Müller joked coldly. Frau Dickmann snorted. It was very convenient, though, that the apartments had the same layout, so that all the furnishings could sit in their places, and nothing would need to be adjusted. Rather than being side by side, the two women were going to live either side of an elderly gentleman by the name of Kunze. He had invited them in for coffee and cake, told jokes constantly and, as they were leaving, said to them, 'I don't know which one of you I am going to fall in love with more.'

Frau Müller put aside a bottle of elderberry cordial to take to Herr Kunze next week when she moved in. She took another one over the fence to Oma Kübler. Oma Kübler was lying asleep in a hammock under the verandah of her bungalow, wearing only underpants and one of her husband's old shirts. 'Eh?' she shouted when Frau Müller called her name. But upon waking, she took hold of Frau Müller's arm and insisted she join her for a mid-afternoon beer. 'It doesn't do to drink alone,' Oma Kübler said. It was still so hot, Oma Kübler was parched, a tall glass of cold beer was just the thing. She had probably been sleeping off the last ones, Frau Müller thought.

'Will you keep this allotment?' Oma Kübler asked. Frau Müller felt tears starting as she shrugged. This place had been like a home for so long. There was the little pond with the miniature cypresses and the gnomes that her late husband had put in. The seat he'd built himself. 'This place is worse and worse with all the aeroplanes, all the dust,' Oma Kübler complained. 'I am afraid every time I pick my kale, it's covered in jet exhaust. There must be somewhere better, closer to your new place.'

Frau Müller changed the topic and asked after Oma Kübler's grandchildren. Oh, the devils. They had made another mess there last weekend with beer bottles and cigarette butts. She should stop letting them use the place, but it was hard to say no. Then last Sunday, Marie Fleischer's father had come round and pinned Oskar against a wall and yelled at him, poor boy. He'd read Marie's diary, in which she'd detailed her excruciating heartbreak, Oskar having dropped her after a couple of months of frenetic sex and false promises. Oma Kübler sighed. Boys. Marie was fifteen. She would meet more of them.

Herr Rabe was moving boxes downstairs to a truck when he noticed a couple around his age outside Martin Engel's door. Martin's parents had come to dispatch his belongings. They gave Herr Rabe a cursory greeting and returned their eyes to the carpet. The worst thing that can happen to a parent had happened. There was nothing for it now but to discard, donate, pack up. Herr Rabe watched them carrying a dead maidenhair fern and a near-dead African violet down the stairs.

Herr Rabe had written to his son. His son had written back. He had a wife named Anja, four daughters and a son. Herr Rabe felt furious. Five children was excessive! The planet could not cope with so many people. Vasectomies should be compulsory after the second birth. Herr Rabe and his former wife had agreed on one child. That was back in the DDR days, when women weren't allowed to stay home for more than three months. Herr Rabe told his son these things in his ongoing correspondence. Jürgen Schulz had given him a reconditioned laptop and taught him how to send emails. Jürgen had a job for the time being and had been sleeping in a loft at his workplace, but intended to keep his apartment. 'I know it's bad,' he said, 'but I'm not superstitious. Martin was unhappy and he killed himself. He picked a bad time of year. He wouldn't have wanted to put us out.'

But Herr Rabe was moving, and much further away than Frau Dickmann and Frau Müller. He was going to the westernmost city in Germany. Just think, after all these years – the West! Herr Rabe laughed as he carried another box of books through the door. Goethe, Gottfried Keller, Thomas Mann and all his long-dead friends were coming with him. Herr Rabe had worked out how to translate his twenty years of misery into digital communications, and his son had understood. He'd written back, telling Herr Rabe he had forgiven him a long time ago. He had called him 'Father'. He had suggested that Herr Rabe come and live with them. And Herr Rabe, in spite of himself, had immediately agreed. Of course it would be terrible. He would hate it. No Konsum. No Dr Fuchs. All the bread wrong, all the names for things different. He would probably fight with his son on a daily basis. But the other option was to remain here, and that was simply worse.

Herr Rabe stacked the boxes in the truck and grumbled at the mover's youth, who was lighting a cigarette in his cupped hands. 'Smoke after the job is done,' Herr Rabe reprimanded him. Oh, that smell – he would never stop loving that smell:

cured, sweet, nicotinic plant, the first faint waft of burning paper. As he glared at the boy, he noticed Frau Kümmel standing against the wall, wearing her slippers and cradling her cat. Herr Rabe had known Frau Kümmel, and her late husband, since his boyhood. He went to kiss her on the cheek, his whiskers pressing into her warm, papery skin. Frau Kümmel's children were going to put her in a nursing home. It was bad, very bad. They did not allow pets. 'Goddamn them,' Herr Rabe sympathised. Frau Kümmel had forgotten where Herr Rabe was going. As he reminded her, he felt a pang of guilt. The Kümmels had been Party faithful, down to the wire. Even in the last few years Frau Kümmel had been seen trundling around the neighbourhood pamphletting for Die Linke.

But she didn't blink. 'A son, a daughter-in-law, and five grandchildren? Give them something from me.' Frau Kümmel smiled, her eyes misted, and she gave Herr Rabe seven kisses.

The girl who shaved the moose

Grace got up early because they were going to the museum. She got ready for school with time to spare. She didn't sprint for the bus. She stood at the end of her driveway, running her shoe through the gravel. She made wave patterns, circles. She picked up a handful of gravel and crunched it in her fingers. She stroked the gate post, its fur of lichen.

The bus pulled up. Whenever she got on the bus, Grace wanted to turn that wheel, pull that lever. She settled herself in a seat halfway down, opened and shut the small window a few times. The bus crunched through the lanes and backroads, sometimes it seemed it might clip the hedges. Greenness rushed past.

They were leaving at playtime. The bell startled Grace out of a daze. She'd been punching holes in a worksheet with the sharpened end of a pencil.

'Hand your sheets back in,' Mr Miles was saying, 'and stand behind your desks.'

Grace looked at her sheet. No one could read a word of it: it was a minefield. Grace wasn't angry, she just hadn't noticed she was doing it.

She pushed the worksheet to the bottom of the pile, walked back to her desk, stood next to her friend Joel. She stood still and quiet, shoulders set, back straight. Joel was wriggling. 'Anna, Riley, Paige, you may go to the bus,' Mr Miles said. Three goody-good girls left the room. Grace kept standing still. Joel kept wriggling. 'Fucking stop wriggling,' Grace said.

Grace and Joel got on the bus last. They sat behind Mr Miles, partly because he'd told them he'd be keeping an eye on them, but also because Grace liked to be near him. He was her favourite teacher ever. There was something gentle about Mr Miles. He never yelled. When he didn't like your behaviour he'd give you a sad look. Mr Miles didn't smile an awful lot, but he always kept his cool.

'Mr Miles has a boyfriend,' someone yelled. It was Caleb.

Grace turned around. 'Shut up or I'll fucking punch you,' she said.

Grace watched Mr Miles's neck as it slowly swivelled. He had chosen to ignore Caleb. 'Grace,' he warned. But she could see that he wasn't angry.

Mr Miles did have a boyfriend, but it wasn't any of Caleb's fucking business.

Grace heard a scuffle behind her. Caleb and Mason were fighting over something. They were a few seats back. Grace saw a glint of silver and Perspex. She thought she knew what it was. But how had they got it?

Grace checked that Mr Miles was looking elsewhere, then dropped to her knees on the bus floor. The old lino was sticky and sandy. 'What are you doing?' Joel said, starting to laugh.

'Shut up.' Grace was little. She could get under the seats. She went between her bag and Joel's, between the legs of Riley and Anna, who squealed, past Georgie and Charlie, and got to Caleb. She rose from under the seat with a fierce look and fell on Caleb with all the force she could summon. The surprise momentarily stunned him. She wrested the thing out of his

112

hand, walked back up the aisle, stood beside Mr Miles's seat and said, 'Here.'

Mr Miles looked into Grace's hand and saw his keyring, with his keys and the tag with a photo of him and Grey on it. He looked into her face, half confused, half accusatory.

'Caleb had it,' she said.

Mr Miles stood up and leaned over the seats. 'Caleb, did you take my keyring?'

'No,' said Caleb, but Mason was giggling and shouting, 'He did! He took it off your desk!' Caleb wrapped his hand over Mason's mouth, and a wrestling match ensued.

Mr Miles looked helpless. 'Wait behind when we get off the bus,' he said. His voice sounded tired.

The man from the museum was teaching them about war. It was easy to get all the wars mixed up. The uniforms were dull. The guns looked like they had never been touched; you couldn't imagine the bayonets red. The young men in the photos had dead looks in their eyes. They weren't dead when the photos were taken, but they were dead shortly afterwards. Or at least, they were dead now. Maybe one or two might be alive, wetting their pants in wheelchairs. It was all very sad, but it was also very boring.

They walked upstairs to another part of the exhibition. Grace looked at the stair rail, how it curved around. It would be fun to slide down. Later, when everyone was doing their worksheets, she could try that. She hung back. The class gathered in a space between two glass cases. Grace stood at a distance and could hardly hear. It was better that way, because she was not listening.

She looked around her. There was an old carriage with a life-size black plastic horse harnessed to it. The harnesses were frozen solid. The horse felt eerily smooth, sounded hollow when she tapped it. On the wall behind her were some heads: a deer, some kind of antelope with long squiggly horns, a moose with enormous craggy antlers. The moose was the best. A good part of its neck was attached, and it leaned out far into the room as if it might bellow over all their heads. Closer, it smelled of cupboards, of fly spray. Its fur was coated in a brittle haze. Fur spray? It was not fresh fur. The moose had been dead over a hundred years. Its eyes were glass, looking at nothing. They reminded Grace of when the home-kill butcher shot the steers. Or when her dad brought back a rabbit from the paddocks, limp and dripping. The eyes open but not seeing. It was creepy.

Grace felt a small shock run through her arm as her hand touched something coarse. Her fingers pushed through the brown bristles. Under the fur, the moose's leather was dry and powdery. She looked at the whale skeleton hanging in the atrium. She heard Mr Miles in the background, talking about medals. Grace was not interested in medals. The sound of his voice was comforting, though. So was the feel of the old dead fur around her fingers as she worked her hand up and down the moose's neck. She reached up to touch its antlers and saw that her hand was hairy.

Grace looked down at her palm with a thrill of horror. There was a hank of fur loose in it. Her fingers closed around it. It felt crunchy. Blood whooshed in her ears. Quite a lot of fur had come away and there was a patch – not exactly a bald patch but a patch of short brown hair, like a mouse's coat – left behind. The hole in the shaggy coat was like a burn or a fungal infection. The moose looked even deader than it had before.

Grace stuffed the fur into her pocket, shuffled closer to the class. What were they meant to be doing now? They were going downstairs. She traipsed after them, back to the bag area. Mr Miles handed out clipboards, each with a worksheet. But she couldn't keep her hand out of her pocket, couldn't stop crumbling the fur through her fingers.

Joel saw her. 'What's in your pocket?' he demanded.

'Nothing.'

'What's in your pocket?'

'Nothing.'

'I said, *what's in your pocket?*'

'Nothing.'

'Come on.'

'Moose fur.'

'Giz a look. Oh, wow. I want some too. Where'd you get it?'

'Upstairs.'

'Show me!'

Grace's whole body tingled with panic as Joel ran up the stairs chanting 'Moose fur, moose fur, moose fur!'

'Stop, Joel!'

He came to the moose. Grace arrived alongside him, panting.

'I can see where you got it from, over here,' Joel said, and started pulling more hair away.

'No – don't, Joel! Don't! We'll get banned from the museum.'

'So? I don't care if I'm banned from the museum.'

'Stop!' Grace reached up to pull Joel's hand away, and then her own hand closed over the moose's neck again.

Grace and Joel stood there, methodically, systematically, stroking the moose. Until all along one side of its neck there was no fur left.

*

Grace felt sick. Both her pockets were stuffed full of fur. Both Joel's pockets were too. Joel was going to take his home, put some in a box that used to have chocolates in it and give the rest to his little brother. Grace didn't know what to do. She couldn't go home like this. She couldn't even go back to school. Mr Miles would see in her face that she had stroked a moose and souvenired its coat.

She needed to pee. She left her clipboard and pencil on a table in the atrium and slunk off to the toilets. In the cubicle, the first thing she did was un-pocket the moose fur and shove it all into the sanitary bin. The little trapdoor fuzzed with brown hairs. It was sticky with something womanly and unknown. They'd had the period talk at school, boys had twirled tampons around their heads and held them under taps and thrown them across the playground. Someone had stuck a pad to the back of Paige's jersey. Grace didn't know what it would be like, to have blood coming out of there. She was both afraid of and excited by the prospect.

It was quiet and safe for a few moments. Then someone came in, banging doors, ripping out paper towels and casting them across the floor. Grace felt everything dry up. I'll wait till she's gone, she thought. She waited. The noise continued. Mr Miles is going to notice I've been in here ages, she thought. What was worse – peeing within someone's hearing or getting told off for lurking?

Grace slid open the lock, walked out gingerly. It was Jenna, twice her natural size in a black down jacket. 'You were in there ages,' Jenna said, not looking at Grace directly. 'You constipated or something?'

Grace turned furious red and went to the washbasin, turned the tap on. Jenna edged up beside her. There was a cake of soap in a tray. It was off-white and had deep grooves of dirt where it had dried and cracked.

'Lick the soap or you love Cameron,' said Jenna.

'Oh, yuck,' said Grace. Cameron dribbled. He wore the same trackpants all week. He lived on a dairy farm and came to school with cow shit on his clothes. No one could love Cameron.

Jenna slid her arm around Grace's neck, pushed her down to the sink. *'Lick the soap.'*

There was nothing Grace could do. She licked the soap.

When Mr Finch walked in and said 'Somebody', you knew you'd have to dig your fingernails into your palms or you'd crack up. You knew you'd have to concentrate on not going red, because if you did, he'd think it was you. 'Somebody has been *wetting* little clumps of toilet paper and *throwing* them at the ceiling.' You'd start to shake, maybe a snort would escape your nose. Or worse: '*Somebody* has done a number *two* in the boys' *urinal*!'

'Somebody,' said Mr Finch, 'has compromised our school's reputation on the trip to the museum yesterday.'

Grace felt a hotness filling her chest, spreading up through her neck, down her arms. Mr Finch knew.

'We have had a long and positive relationship with the museum,' he went on, 'but I'm not sure if we'll be welcome back after yesterday.' He paused and looked around the cluster of faces, searching each one for a twitch of muscle, a blush of guilt. No one moved. 'Because *somebody*,' he went on, 'or some of *you*, took it into their heads that it would be a good idea to *shave* the *fur* off of a *moose.*'

Around the room there were stirrings of mirth. Grace didn't feel like laughing this time. It was more she was pinching herself so she didn't cry. She and Joel had agreed not to say anything, but what if he did? Joel was a blurter. And they hadn't shaved it! Why did Mr Finch think they'd shaved it? Grace thought of her mum's razors, pink and stubbly on the rim of the bath. She remembered the time she'd shaved her arms, out of curiosity, and cut painful nicks in her skin. Why would anyone want to shave anything? She would leave it all to grow. Every time she looked between her legs, it was furrier there. It was comforting. Why would anyone bring a razor to the museum?

Mr Finch's glare panned the room. Everyone was quiet except Riley, who hiccupped, almost a laugh. Grace's whole body felt like it was filled with poison. She would be told off in front of everyone. Her parents would have to come in. She'd have to replace the moose. Where would you even get a moose from? Were there any mooses in New Zealand? Did a moose live in the open or deep in the forest? Were mooses dangerous? Grace imagined being tossed high in the air on those big, blunt antlers, or pressed against a rock by an angry bull moose.

'I see,' said Mr Finch, still staring. 'No one is going to own up. In that case, the whole class will be held responsible.'

A groan rippled around the room. The children imagined hours of detention, watching the light through the stained classroom curtains getting dimmer and greyer as they stayed writing lines. What moved in a school after dark? Late for gymnastics. Missing out on games. Getting out of setting the table, but detention was worse.

'You will each write a letter this lunchtime,' Mr Finch said. 'You will apologise for damaging a museum exhibit. And you will promise to be sensible visitors in the future.' He nodded to Mr Miles, folded his hands behind him, and walked out.

Was that all?

'When you have finished your letter,' said Mr Miles, 'you may go to lunch. Use a clean sheet of refill. Remember how to do letter layout.' He picked out his favourite blue whiteboard marker and neatly wrote a prompt across the clean white space. That was another good thing about Mr Miles. His stuff was always nice. His board was never smeary.

Across the table, Anna and Riley were writing in glitter ink. Anna drew a picture of herself and a penguin. Joel's head was close to the desk and he was breathing hard. Joel hated writing. Grace looked at the blank paper and her stomach twisted. She felt in her pencil tin for her compass, touched the sharp point, concentrated on working on her desk hole. She poked it a little more each day. She was nearly right through.

One by one the students took their letters up to Mr Miles's desk. Mr Miles was eating a sandwich and looked uncomfortable. He was missing his lunchtime too. But what could she say? I am very sorry, it was me who shaved the moose. But not with a razor. Just with my hand. I am sorry. I love the museum.

Joel pushed his chair in with a loud smack. 'See you at the stump,' he said, walking away. Grace and Joel always ate their lunch on top of the stump. It was fun to pull off bits of bark, look for bugs underneath. Joel said if he found a huhu grub, he'd eat it. Was he going to say anything? Would he own up? If he didn't, should she? Then it would all be her. She would get in all the trouble.

It was only Grace and Mr Miles in the room now. 'How are you getting on there, Grace?' he asked, sounding tired again.

'Nearly done.' Quickly and messily, she copied down the prompt. She added *I am very sorry about the moose.* That was honest. She drew a moose head with a big smile, front on, antlers wide. She coloured it brown. She lifted the piece of paper off her desk, walked across the carpet.

'Here,' she said, sliding her letter into the middle of the pile.

'Thanks, Grace.' Mr Miles was looking at the clock.

Grace stood there. 'Um.'

'And Grace.'

'Yes?'

'About my keyring. Thank you.'

'Oh. That's OK.'

'I'd have had a hard time starting my car without my keys.' Mr Miles forced a smile. He looked like he wanted to start his car and drive a million miles away and never drive back. 'But no swearing next time, OK?'

'OK.'

'And don't be too rough on those boys. You might hurt them.' It was a real smile now. Grace thought about this. She was smaller, but she was a good fighter.

Quietly, she said, 'It was me.'

'Sorry?'

'It was me who stroked the moose. I didn't mean to, but its fur came off in my hand.'

'You didn't mean to stroke it?'

'No. I mean, not really, but . . .'

The real smile again. 'It must have been a pretty good stroke.'

'Mr Miles?'

'Yes, Grace.'

'How much detentions will I have?'

'No detention.'

'But it was me.'

Mr Miles was lifting his satchel, about to sling it over his shoulder. It was a soft black leather. 'I believe you,' he said. 'But I can't prove it.'

'So am I in trouble?'

'Yes.'

'So can I ever go back to the museum?'

'Yes. Grace, I have to meet a friend. Go have your lunch.'

Grace watched him slide in his chair, stared at him.

'Go have your lunch,' he repeated. 'I'm locking up in 5 . . . 4 . . . 3 . . . 2 . . .'

Grace ran to the door. The carpet was air. She felt . . . she didn't know what she felt. She jerked the zip of her backpack, closed her hand around her drink bottle, dragged out the bread bag with her lunch in it. The playground was full of screams. The sky was a painful white.

Sin City

Predictably, halfway through the second round of drinks, Margot excused herself and went to the toilet. Shortly afterwards, Gregor went to stretch his legs. The bathroom door was locked for a long time. Bill, a small man with a proportionately small bladder, went and pissed off the porch. Next to me, the new woman squirmed uncomfortably. I'd been watching her sideways for half an hour and could see she was terrified.

I pictured Margot and Gregor. I don't know why – they weren't worth picturing. Her over the basin, loose tits swinging. It was all Gregor's idea to begin with, the parties, and for no better reason than that he was already fucking Margot. It was often at Arthur's place because Arthur had put in a deck and a Jacuzzi. Arthur was a lawyer and he could afford that shit. He could afford that shit the way Bill, who was a groundsman, could afford tinned beans. Arthur had been divorced twice, two kids with each, and was now married to Jean. One brat.

I was pretending to listen to Roger, who'd been a regular for a while (president of the tennis club), and to the husband of the terrified woman. I'd forgotten his name, and hers, immediately. What were these men talking about? Golf? The stock exchange? Drunk Muldoon and the snap election? Not sex. No one ever talked about sex. Your best friend could be loudly fucking your wife in the adjacent toilet, and it'd be How about this weather.

That was the odd thing. It was all about sex, and at the same time, it wasn't. We did all this to prove to ourselves, to each other, that sex was nothing. In any case, I wasn't listening.

There she was, in the centre of things, so cool, so demure, the most beautiful woman in the world. She looked like Princess Diana, right down to the haircut and the dreamy blue eyes, only more lovely. Everything she did was an artwork: placing a bowl of chips on the table, adjusting the volume knob on the record player. She was wearing a long blue dress her ankles barely escaped, but when she bent down the polyester fabric clung to her lovely arse.

She was polite. 'How are you this evening, Adam?' she asked me. I was on my feet, pretending to sway to the music, wine glass in hand, but really I wanted to be near her. She spoke with a soft smile, like this was just a regular soirée. Husband's at-home for everyone from the office. It was as if it didn't pain her. I knew that it did: to be thrown among pigs every second Friday, to be put into the collective pool and fished out. Jean was a jewel and didn't belong in with that dross. Oh, it was all right for titsy Margot, who'd been a slut since fourteen and must have fucked every man in town by now. It was all right for dried-up Carol, who'd hardly say good morning to me anymore – she deserved to go and suck dicks. But Jean, although a mother, looked like a virgin. She was twenty-three and the rest of us were in our forties. It was impossible not to want to rescue her.

Gregor appeared in the kitchen; Margot flopped down beside her husband on the leather couch. I could have sworn I heard her squelch. I nodded to Gregor as he cracked open a stubby, and made for the toilet myself. About this time of the evening, every time, I began to lose composure. I began to feel the blood rushing to my cheeks, an unpleasant twist in my groin, part lust and part hate. I wanted, and wanted to kill at the same time. I lifted the seat and pissed in the bowl. It felt like sacrilege, pissing in Jean's toilet, my half-cut slash where she'd make her pretty tinkle. I'd piss on anything of Arthur's, but since she'd married him and redecorated the house, the bathroom felt like hers. Her scents lining the mirror, her hand crème on the vanity, the sponge by the bathtub that got to caress her skin. I looked at the peach-coloured towels and wondered if Gregor had wiped his end on any of them. Disgusted with myself, I filled my cupped palms and splashed my face. The cold water made me feel firmer. In the mirror, I saw a man who wasn't bad for forty-seven. Arthur had always been the smarter one, but I, admittedly, was the better-looking. It wasn't that Arthur was ugly, but after forty, if a man doesn't have much to start with, he won't have much to go on. I allowed myself to admire my hair, still chestnut, still lining my forehead except for two triangles at the temples; my jaw, still defined; my teeth and the whites of my eyes, reasonably white. If there was any one of us Arthur's wife ought to be content to be shared with, I reasoned, logically, it would be me.

But that was the problem. Every time, the last four or five parties, she'd conjured up tricks to make sure she'd go home with Bill. I had never had a chance on her. Gregor had, maybe once, and Roger, and I think Ron. Why Bill? I knew, and I suppose everyone else did, that she was fixing things, that she'd put some identifying mark on his keys, or who knows what. No one had said anything up until now. But it was going too far. If it happened again tonight, I promised my reflection, I would do something about it.

What? I didn't hate Bill. I hated him with a passion, but I didn't hate him. In my mind he was still a boy: slow to read, late to mature, quietly spoken and always on the outer of things. On the other hand, he combed his hair to one side, wore V-neck cardigans and corduroy pants like an old man. He may even have worn orthotic shoes. In the lounge, I seated myself beside him. There was something comforting about his effeminate face, his greying curls. He was a man who reassured you of your own manhood. But what could he do for a twenty-three-year-old bombshell?

I watched him, and I could tell he wasn't watching her. He was talking to me softly about his boss or his orchid house or something. There was definitely something going on. He was avoiding her deliberately. They were having a real affair. Perhaps he was meeting her outside of all this. Perhaps she'd drop round to the school or sportsground or wherever he worked mowing lawns and picking up rubbish, and they'd have a quickie in the caretaker's cottage. Perhaps she'd bake him a batch of scones. Did she have a thing for short men, curly-haired men, men with diminutive chins? There was no explaining some people's preferences.

Now it was time for the bowl. The new woman, whose name was Maureen, apparently, had to go first. She was shaking like a hundred-year-old. She got my keys and looked at me wide-eyed and afraid. I had to play by the rules. I stood up, quite normally. 'Well, come on love,' I said, and drew my arm around her, guiding her into the hall.

Once we were out of earshot, I said, 'Look, I know you don't want to do this.'

'Oh, no, really, it's fine,' she said. She had one of those very girly, high voices. She'd trained herself never to speak too deep. Carol, my wife, had a tendency to growl. Jean had a moderately pitched voice, but soft.

'You don't want to do it. And as a matter of fact, I'm not in the mood myself, tonight.'

Her mouth was open slightly, and she was staring at my tie-pin. 'It's not that there's anything wrong with you, hon,' I said, touching her bare arm. Another night, or another lifetime, maybe, I would have. 'I'm just tired and grumpy and I want to sleep.'

Her relief fell on us, massive and warm. Tears blurred her mascara, and the tip of her nose turned red. 'Thank you,' she whispered. 'This was my husband's idea. Don't think I'm a . . . a . . .'

I felt nice for a moment. 'Whatever it is,' I reassured her, 'you're not one.' Then the nasty feeling I'd had all evening resurfaced. Viciousness rumbled in my stomach, and I couldn't keep a lid on it. 'If you don't like it, why did you come?'

'I don't know.'

'Get a divorce.' I shrugged and opened the door for her.

I walked around Arthur's garden, smelled something sweet, heard the night wind slapping leaves. I sat on the back porch for a while and watched the sky get darker. Arthur's house looked out over the town. I could have fooled myself it was a nice place, with all those lights twinkling and the darkness swallowing up all those squat state houses and ugly Victorian buildings. It wasn't nice. We all lived here by pure bad luck. I was feeling too sober to look at it, so I got up and slunk back inside. Let anyone ask questions, if they even noticed. There was no one in the hall, no one in the lounge. There were various bottles of spirits at various stages of emptiness sitting on top of the cocktail cabinet, but I couldn't find a clean glass. My heart was pounding. I found myself padding up the thickly carpeted stairs. I would go and find Bill and Jean and ask what the hell they thought they were doing, but first I would go and tell Arthur, my childhood best friend, that he was a complete and utter fuckwit. It wouldn't be the first time. He wouldn't give a hoot.

Some kind of shitty hit-parade was blaring from a radio, but I could still hear other sounds above it. I pushed open the bedroom door and peered in. The bedside lamps were on. There was something of an orgy happening in the king-size waterbed. By the looks of things, Roger and Arthur were spit-roasting Ron's wife, Sandra. I thought I could make out the dark shape of Ron masturbating in the corner, but perhaps it was the curtain moving in the breeze. Jean's sweet curtains, and her bed, and her sheets. 'This is bad, this is wrong,' I yelled, but they were too preoccupied to notice. I went back downstairs, glared into the kitchen, where two women were making out against the wall oven, blouses off, flesh squeezing around their bra straps. Once upon a time such sights would have got me going, but now I didn't care. I found my keys in my jacket pocket, slammed the front door, went to my car. Perhaps I would have a heart attack before I got there.

But I didn't head straight to Bill's. I drove to the Commercial and parked around the back. This town was like sticking your head under a guillotine blade, every second. This town was like drinking shitshakes. It was mind-numbing, soul-numbing, heart-killing. It was like a black-and-white TV in an old folks' home, screen filled with static, with all the old folks passed out in their chairs, dreaming of their regrets. They'd dreamed of everything and done nothing. People called this place 'Sin City' and added 'Vegas' as a suffix to its name, well that was a fucking joke. It wasn't wild or debaucherous or sinful. There was no casino here. It was just a tired, sad backwater. I walked across the damp carpet to the bar and imagined dropping a nuclear warhead on the whole place. From far away, the mushroom cloud would be so beautiful.

The new prime minister was making noises about the country becoming nuclear free. I would need to act promptly.

'One dirty martini, please,' I said to the barman. He looked affronted. He wasn't used to anyone saying please or ordering anything other than Lion Brown. He looked up at the rows of dusty bottles on the shelves behind him. I didn't watch – I knew he'd be mixing something rotten with something awful.

He handed me something in a smeary glass. It was yellowy, like urine. I smelled the pineapple before I tasted it.

'Excuse me,' I said, looking him in the eye, 'but what is this?'

'Dirty martini.'

'A dirty martini doesn't have pineapple in it.'

'Doesn't it?' He looked unconcerned. I knew he wouldn't make me another one. I knocked it back in one vomitous swill and ordered a Lion Brown. Fuck everything.

I looked around the room. There was a guy with a long grey beard and a Swanndri swaying alone in the middle of the floor. He looked like something out of Barry Crump. There was a collection of sad fucks losing their hair, throwing darts at the beat-up board in the corner. The wall around it was peppered with drunken misses. Someone's greasy head lay on the pool table, cue clenched in slumped fist. There were two women in the place: one sitting alone looking fed-up, one in leather and lace leaning on the bar. I was pretty sure she was a hooker, but it was hard to tell with fashions nowadays. That whore, Madonna. The leather-clad woman saw me watching and shuffled towards me. I looked down – impossible not to, when you are six foot six – and saw a wrinkled abyss between her breasts. On either side of it, skin shifted and sweated. When she opened her mouth to talk to me, I saw she had no teeth. I couldn't understand a word she was saying.

She leaned in closer. Oh God, I thought, sorry love, I'd rather hang myself in the dunny than pay you for sex. She made a sibilant sound. I drank deep from the piss-warm liquid in my glass. She made the sound again.

'Cigarette,' she was saying. 'Cigarette.' With a relief almost equal to Maureen's earlier that evening, I pulled a box of tailor-mades from my pocket, stuck one between her gums and lit it. Her face smoothed over, and she breathed serenely, like a baby. She sat on her stool with her back to the barman, smoking and not saying a word. This was as close to bliss as she'd ever get. Maybe she'd have her way with the bearded swayer later on, maybe she wouldn't. A toothless woman would be good for giving head. I downed the rest of my beer and left.

A neat box hedge went down either side of Bill's path. There were leadlight windows either side of his door and a terracotta dog by the mat. I pounded with my fist, felt sweat rise in it. I wasn't expecting an answer, thought I'd have to go round and pound on the bedroom window for a while, but in moments there was a shuffle in the hallway and Bill appeared, fully clothed, in his sheepskin slippers. His reading glasses sat halfway down his nose. Peering over them, he looked perplexed. 'Adam,' he said, in a friendly voice. 'Come in.'

Would joining in whatever they were doing be a consolation? I thought of Roger and Arthur like animals in the bed. They had no qualms about anything, those men. Arthur would go into court and defend the most violent rapist like he was simply a man going about his daily business, doing no harm to anyone. He had reasoned away any moral sensibilities by the age of seventeen. 'We are all machines,' he'd told me once, when we were smoking on the roof of his parents' shed. Computers would one day take over the world. I didn't want to live in that world. No, I would not join Bill and Jean. I would simply say my piece and leave. Perhaps then she would realise how I loved her.

I meekly followed Bill to the lounge. The lights were on, the old black-and-white TV was blaring. A cup of tea, half drunk, sat on the sad tiled coffee table.

'Can I get you a drink of something?' Bill asked. It struck me that Bill had been born an old man. I sat in the armchair opposite him, not knowing what to say. Perhaps she was about to appear, a vision in a negligee or transparent dressing gown. Perhaps she'd be horrified to see me sitting there.

The TV went on and on, the kettle boiled in the kitchen. Bill knew how I liked my tea. He brought it to me on a saucer, with a gingernut beside it. Bill was a decent man and Margot had never deserved him.

We sat and drank our tea in silence, but it was companionable. Minutes ticked by and no woman appeared. 'You're home alone,' I observed, after a while.

Bill nodded, draining his cup and placing it on the table. 'Same as every time.' I studied his face, waiting. He smiled. 'God, you didn't really think she'd be interested in me, did you? I'm just a way out.'

'Where does she go, then?'

'To her mother's.'

That made sense. Did her mother – the same age as, if not younger than, Arthur and Bill and Gregor and me – know what her daughter's marriage had become? Was Jean's wedding picture on that mantelpiece, her slim and stunning, him the Cheshire cat? Was his money enough to make up for his behaviour?

'It's the little boy.'

I had forgotten about him. Arthur never spoke about any of his children. They were products of his personal machine.

How old was the little one now?

'He's only just two, can't say Margot ever would have left ours overnight at that age. She might act the tart, Adam, but Jean's a lovely mother. She dotes on that boy.'

I felt incensed at his calling Jean a tart, but settled for turning red and saying nothing.

'The first night she came here . . .' He gave a long sigh. 'I wanted to, of course, but I just couldn't, you know.' He paused. 'My pecker played up.'

This was remarkably candid.

'She cried, and I thought it was because of me. What man wouldn't be able to make love to a woman like that? And so I asked her to talk, and I just listened. She wasn't even remotely fussed about my shortcomings, Adam. She told me her baby was sleeping at her mother's, and she missed him. So I got dressed and drove her around there. After that, we made a deal. She'd pick my keys, I'd drop her off, and I'd have a quiet one at home. Can't say I mind too much.'

He didn't mention Margot, but I read her in his face. I slurped the last of my tea. 'Do you have a nip of anything stronger?' I asked.

Bill pulled a bottle of sherry from the cupboard beside the TV, and two glasses that looked like something my mother would own, deep in her caches of never-used homewares. He poured us each a generous tipple, and we drank. We drank again. The late show finished, and the test patterns came on. We sat looking at the test patterns and drinking that foul sweet sherry.

'Adam,' Bill said, 'I love you.'

I remembered how we'd been boys together, taking the long way home, poking in streams with sticks. I remembered how his hair had been curly and golden. He'd been the hobbit and I'd been Gandalf. He'd always been small and girlish; I'd always been stupidly tall. I looked at him disapprovingly.

He sighed, setting his glass down. 'You've been my friend forever, and I love you. I love them all – Arthur, Gregor, Roger even. And the ladies, but you fellers most of all.'

'Let's get out of here,' I said. 'Let's pack the car and fuck off and leave our wives and leave this shit-awful town. We'll die here, Bill.'

'We'll die wherever we are.' Bill shrugged.

'We'll die here quicker. Come on. You know you hate it all as much as I do.'

Bill sipped. 'I can't. Jono's got footy in the morning. And I can't just not turn up at the firm on Monday.'

'Firm? What firm?'

'The insurance firm. Where I work.'

'You're a fucking groundsman.'

Bill sighed. 'I haven't been a groundsman in five years, Adam. I sell insurance.'

'You're always talking about plants.'

'Gardening is my hobby.'

'Oh.' Perhaps he was right. I hoped he wouldn't suggest we look at his orchids. I would kill myself if I had to look at Bill's orchids. It was too dark, I reasoned. Bill wouldn't show me his orchids by torchlight. Or would he? Did he have lighting installed in the orchid house?

'The problem with you, Adam,' said Bill, 'is that you live in your own head. You don't care what happens to anyone else.'

'That's not true. I came here tonight because I care about somebody.'

'No, you don't. You just want the same thing from her any of the rest of them want.'

I was too drunk to be angry. Bill's eyes were closing. He

132

wasn't angry, either. I looked at the test patterns, that horrific rainbow. How anyone could watch the test patterns and not want to die, I didn't know. I would leave. I didn't care whether anyone else would or not. I would leave this place, and that bitch Carol, and my rude, pimply daughter who was bound to turn out mean and ugly. Our son had made a break for it years ago.

Pressed into the vinyl armchair, I imagined myself driving. I turned out of Bill's street and headed up the hill on the highway west. I drove past a church and another church and a gas station, closed and dark. I drove past a closed pub. I drove on to the next town, where everything was, of course, closed. Hardly a neon light flashed in a dim window. I drove to the town after that, and it was the same again, although this one had traffic lights. I stopped at the red, and sat and waited for nothing, and nothing came, and after an eternity the light went green. I took the coastal road and drove around the sea. It was dark, and I was drunk, and I couldn't make out any beaches. I knew they were there: some rocky, some with sheer cliffs, some sand-blasting hollows where people surfed and picnicked and fucked and holidayed out of pure desperation. I knew on my right there were paddocks filled with dormant cows, their udders slowly filling with milk. It wouldn't be long before the farmers'd be up and out into the paddocks, driving them to the sheds. I thought about the sea slopping on my left. I wondered what the sea was doing at this time of night.

When I was a young man, and Carol was still kind and beautiful, there'd been this dolphin up north. It came into the Hokianga and swam with people, took kids for rides and bounced balls off its nose. We sat on the pier with crowds of other young people, scantily clad, laughing, ridiculously leggy and sun-tanned. We were nineteen and we'd run away to get married. Her folks didn't like me, or, more specifically, they didn't like my folks. That's where I wanted to drive to: Hokianga in the nineteen-fifties. I was a young man; Jean wasn't even born. I wouldn't have to worry about her. I could find that dolphin or, after it was dynamited, another motherfucking dolphin.

I managed to stretch out my leg to turn off the TV with my toe. The rainbow died. The resultant darkness was a kind of quiet. I was somewhere in the middle of the coastal road and I had run out of gas. I hadn't been keeping an eye on the needle, and anyway, the gauge was wonky. I let the car putter to a halt on the grass verge. I let the armchair tip back, the footrest extend. Soon I would be asleep. I'd be passed out in Bill's lounge. I'd be asleep in my car on the coastal road in the middle of nowhere, and when the farmers finished milking I'd still be asleep. Families would pass on their way to and from sports games; utes would pass with dogs barking on the tray. Bill's youngest son would arrive in the lounge in his football uniform and find us both asleep in yesterday's clothes. I'd wake up stinking, with a trail of drool from my mouth to the hot vinyl upholstery. I'd open the passenger door and feel the assault of the sea breeze and freeze my dick off taking a leak. I might vomit, and find Carol's handkerchief in the glove box and wipe my mouth. I'd vomit in Bill's toilet and scrub up the mess. I'd walk down the path to my car. I'd walk to the nearest house. I'd beg a few litres of fuel, enough to get me to the next town, where I could fuel up properly. That would be what I would do. I'd be asleep soon. I'd be asleep in a chair next to Bill asleep in a chair. The sky was growing creamy. Everything that had happened in the past twelve hours was a tremendous joke.

Trashing the flowers

The flowers smell like sick. They sit in the middle of the table, quiet and ostentatious. There's that kind of lily they put in the church when someone dies, some greenery that might be magnolia leaves, some plastic-looking gerberas, their stems strengthened with green wire. All wrapped up in layers of soft green and white plastic, stems in a pottle of water.

'You know what we do with flowers here?' Ariana says.

'What?' Laura fingers her car keys, wondering where to leave them. At home on the hall table, she had a brass plate with a dragon etched into it. All the keys went there.

'We trash them.'

'Oh, OK.' The flowers go on stinking.

'Want us to help you with those?'

Laura looks around, as if there might be a suitcase on each side of her she's forgotten about. The flowers – she means the flowers, she realises. She doesn't know what to say. She fingers her keys some more. 'Maybe later,' she says, quietly, at length. 'Maybe later I will.'

Later, the kids asleep, the dishes done, she sees the bouquet again. It's been blurred out and now it resurfaces. It doesn't seem odd that he's bought her flowers. Even though it's only the second time ever, the first being the day he lost his job. They had no guaranteed income and he'd gone and spent seventy bucks on the flowers she'd longed for off and on for twelve years. She was mad at him. And now this, when it's too late for anything, sent to her work. Laura feels a sense of panic looking at the bouquet, like it might be able to spy on her, relay messages back to him. She's in the kitchen now. She's boiling the jug. She's wearing a grey blouse and a black skirt. There wasn't a card with the flowers. She hopes there's been a mistake, that they were meant for someone else. Or that they've come from her mother. But her mother, hundreds of kilometres away, doesn't know what's happened.

The kitchen feels like a staffroom. It's clean and not too run-down. All the mugs are impersonal; the jars holding teabags, instant coffee and Milo all match. There's a printed canvas above the sink that says 'Love Smile Happiness Fun' in different fonts on a background of uterine red. Laura watches the tea bag infuse, pulls it out quickly with pinched thumb and forefinger. There doesn't seem to be a compost bucket. She drops it in the bin, watches brown run down the white plastic liner, steam rise up. She watches a cat walking along the fence. There's something funny about that cat: it's wobbly, it's oddly shaped. It's pregnant, she realises. Tears spring to her eyes.

Karen and one of her sons are watching TV, slumped on the couch. The other son is in an armchair, fingers darting around a hand-held device. Waves of concentration move over his face as he shoots stuff or blows stuff up. Karen's face looks the same as it does every day: old, tired, strained. Karen can't be much older than me, thinks Laura. But there's a resignation in Karen that Laura hasn't felt in herself. A practical haircut. Old purple Chuck Taylors with holes in the sides.

'I don't need to be in the safe house,' Laura had told Cheryl at Refuge. 'I don't want to take up a room when there are people who need it more.'

Cheryl looked back at her, unwavering, intent. 'The safe house is there for women who need to leave abusive homes,' she said, in her gentle explaining voice. 'It's not a matter of a hierarchy or whose situation is the worst. And there's more than one safe house in town.'

Laura nodded, holding a mug of instant coffee someone in the office had made her. It was lukewarm and very sweet.

'So the question is, do you feel safe at home?'

'Yes and no. I mean, no.'

'You don't feel safe at home. You want to leave.'

Laura nodded, teeth bared. She was already crying, but those four words made the tears roll faster. *You want to leave.* It was so simple and so impossible.

'He never hits me. I mean. He does hit the kids, but . . . I guess that isn't safe, is it?'

'What were you telling me, about sleeping? Or, not sleeping?'

'That I'm scared to go to bed.'

'Laura.'

'Yes.'

'Why are you scared to go to bed?'

Her face was wet, and she couldn't talk.

'Laura?'

'I'm scared I'll be raped.'

'Has he raped you before?'

Laura looked at the ceiling, at the basket of dolls, at the thank-you cards on the wall. All those effusions from all those women. Thank you, you have saved my life. I don't know where I'd be without you. Thank you from the bottom of my heart. 'I don't know if it was rape.'

She had lain there on the bed, unable to move. If I don't move, she thought to herself, it's like it isn't happening to me.

It is happening to this person, this thing, that is lying here not moving. But if I don't move, I am not in this thing. To lie there not moving, in the body that's been yours since birth, in the body that was delivered safely into the world and held in your mother's arms, and your father's, and washed and dressed and fed and grown. The body that could high-jump, could run, could stilt-walk, could do ballet, swim, bend, stretch, dance, fall over drunk, dive, hike, climb, make love. To be in that body but not in it, and naked, and it doesn't matter that the sheets are off and that you are lying still and that you are cold. To see the person you'd thought you loved, the person you'd made children with, who'd seen you labour and give birth and breastfeed and stagger up in the night and soothe and clean up shit and puke, and cuddle and rock and sing to and read stories to, and tell stories, and cook, who'd seen you do all those things. To see that person take your body and enter it as if you were not in it, as if it were a kayak or a jacket that belonged to him. You see his face and the lines on his forehead, and his dark eyebrows, and all you feel for him is a cold, cold hatred, deep in your groin, spreading upwards. You hate this man and you are going to leave him. This is the last time he will ever do this.

That wasn't the only time.

She sits holding her mug, feeling the tea cool inside it. The too-sweet coffee at Refuge, the stale-tasting black gumboot here. All these mugs of warm liquid. All these small ceramic vessels.

Karen and her son stare forward. It's a cooking show. Laura wants to sit down with them, talk to them, but she can't think of how to start the conversation. Imagine if your biggest problem was figuring out how to win a cooking show. Do you like to cook, Karen? But you can't remind her about home. Karen's shoulder's been put out, and Laura doesn't like to ask her if it was him or something else. Karen's long white legs stick out of long denim shorts. Laura feels like a middle-class bitch among these women. Work clothes, heels, pantyhose, makeup. The other two wear uniforms of denim and polar fleece. She's seen Karen's bras hanging out to dry on the line, the underwires poking through, the white lace yellowed. She feels awful for having new, matching underwear. In the daze after leaving, she went on something of a shopping spree. It was a way of saying stuff you. It was a way of making herself new again, encasing this body in something that had never touched another body. She bought a new lipstick and some nice moisturiser, a skirt, some new pants, new shoes and three sets of lingerie: ivory, pink and black. Then she realised that she was out of cash, that her part-time income was a lot less than the full-time income Craig had, now he had a job again, and that it would be stretched just buying food and petrol and clothes for the kids. She didn't know how to ask about child support.

The day they arrived, Aroha from Refuge showed her where to put their bags. They have a small double room with a decent-sized window. They have a single wardrobe with five hangers in it. The kids' uniforms don't need hanging: they are folded and put in the small Melteca chest of drawers with peeling corners. She hangs up her two skirts, two blouses and a dress, sorts the rest of her clothes into piles in an open suitcase on the floor. Did she bring enough of everything? Once, in a fit of environmentalism, she wrote a list titled 'Items I need'. It was minimalist: three pairs of underwear (one on, one spare, one in the wash), two bras (one light, one dark), one pair long pants, one pair shorts. Now she looks at similar numbers of items, thinks perhaps she won't manage on that.

There's a big black sack in the lounge: a playcentre has donated some clothing. Maternity pants, oh God. Some kids' stuff, stained down the front, that looks too small for hers. Baby onesies stretched horizontally in the wash, necks gaping. Bibs. A few dresses that look tired and out of date. Miserably, she acknowledges to herself she wouldn't be seen dead in those. Neither would Ariana or Karen, she suspects. She folds the clothes and returns them to the sack, props it in the corner. Maybe someone else will turn up and need these things.

Ariana is off to train for a fight. She's a Muay Thai kickboxer. Her kids are asleep, like Laura's. Laura and Karen will keep an ear out.

'She beat me, last time,' Ariana says. 'This time, I'm going to do her some damage.'

It hadn't occurred to Laura that one might fight. 'If anyone touches me they're gonna fucking get touched,' Ariana said once, full of swagger. Then she looked pensive and added, almost as an afterthought, 'And after that it gets ugly.'

It wasn't that Ariana wasn't fighting back, it was that she was usually coming out worse off. 'I'm just lucky CYFs didn't take my kids,' she told Laura. 'If I hadn't come here, they probably would've. They took my cousin's four-year-old 'cause her boyfriend was giving her the bash.'

Laura watches Ariana walk to the door in her big puffer jacket, pull on her black skate shoes. She walks out without tying up the laces. Laura hears the car door close and the engine start.

In the double bed, her children are sleeping, one diagonal, one almost horizontal. She wonders how to fit herself around them. She could sleep in one of the bunk beds they've emptied, but she wants to be close to them, hear their breathing, feel

140

their little hearts going. If she moves them, they might wake up. If she sleeps on one side, the other one might want her and complain she's favouring the sibling. She makes up her mind to get in the middle, lifts the bottom edge of the duvet, crawls up.

The duvet is thin polycotton with a nineties geometric pattern. The sheets smell of sadness. Laura thinks wistfully of her childhood when she looks at the décor in this house. What it was to be eleven, to have an imaginary boyfriend who was handsome and kind, the sort who'd help you pull prickles out of your foot, hold your hand, do bombs with you at the public pool. What it was to believe in love, in forever, in happy families, in endless Christmases, in decks, in barbecues, in armchairs. To roll down hills and pick dry grass off your clothes. To snuggle in a sleeping bag in a tent. The feeling of diving into a swimming hole in a cold river, the soft slime of the rocks under your feet. The feeling of standing at the start of the athletics track, watching the official raise the starting pistol. The crack of it. The fire in your thighs as your body springs forward, flings itself into the air. She smells Leighton's head, a familiar tang. She lies awake, eyes open.

She must have fallen asleep, because she finds herself waking and sitting bolt upright. She's kicking and pushing, shouting 'No, no, no!' The kids wake and cry. 'Mama!' Leighton wails. Millie says, 'What are you doing, Mum?'

She's kicked off all the covers, made them cold. She was having the same dream again: Craig is here and he's in the room, he's come to get her. Tonight he was lifting up the duvet the way she had when she got into bed, and he was reaching up for her legs, ready to pull her out onto the floor. She pulls up the covers, heart pounding, snuggles the children into her, one head on each of her shoulders.

In the morning they'll wake and ask the same questions again. Why are we here? Where's Dad? When are we going home? If they're asking about home, how does she even know she's done the right thing? Do they miss him? Even though he'd get home and drink beer in front of the TV, and she was the one who'd do everything for them, and they hardly seemed to notice he was there? Even though he yelled at them when they were noisy and made fun of them when they cried and threw things at them, do they love him?

First there were the texts. *I demand that you come home. Come home and stop this nonsense. I demand to see MY children. You can't do this to me.* And then: *This is illegal.* Is it illegal, she wonders. Is it illegal to go to a safe house? She's been to the lawyers, talked about options. They never mentioned it was illegal. It can't be illegal, that's ridiculous. Maybe there are countries in the world where it is, where taking your children and going into hiding would warrant your death. Technically, Craig is a legal guardian of Leighton and Millie. But it isn't guarding a child, to hit it around the head.

After three days she bought a new SIM card, and the texts stopped. She's always nervous parking her car, walking to a shop. What is she afraid of? That he'll see her and yell at her? That he'll grab her and try to drag her somewhere? How mad is he? Would he, simply, in cold blood, kill her? And now, when she hasn't responded to the nastiness, here comes a bunch of flowers. He's trying to unsettle her. He knows she can't predict which way he'll swing next. It's like all those years they lived together, when he'd come in the front door and her whole being would tense up, not knowing if today he'd be sunshine or storms, if the food she'd made would be vaguely edible or the worst shit he'd ever tasted.

When she was a girl she used to lie awake, not worrying

exactly, just thinking. Her brain would go over things, make up stories, her body would remain alert. Sometimes she'd get up and find her parents and tell them she couldn't sleep. They'd be reading in the lounge or, if it was late, they'd be in their own bed, the room filled with the smell of them and the sound of their quiet breathing. She remembers her father walking her to her room, her hand in his, over the wooden floorboards. 'Stay in your bed, Laura,' he told her. 'Don't worry about sleep. Your body will take the sleep it needs.'

She thinks about that now. If the body could take what it needed, pluck things from the air, soothe itself.

Laura picks Millie up from school. She always uses the side entrance now. She can hide her car in the cul-de-sac and enter the school without being seen. If he looked for her car, he'd probably look for it out the front. She's a little late. Millie has hung her bag and shoes in the branches of a peach tree. She won't come down. 'Come on, Millie,' Laura pleads. 'We have to pick up Leighton from kindy.'

'I'll come in a minute,' Millie says, feet swinging.

Millie's friend Eliza arrives and decides to get up into the tree with her. Eliza's mum sidles up and makes small talk. Laura doesn't know her all that well. In any case, she doesn't know who she can trust. When Eliza's mum asks 'How's things', she replies, 'Oh, good. Just the usual.'

Sometimes lying isn't so bad. Sometimes you have to bend the truth to protect yourself. She holds Millie's hand, guides her out of the branches. 'See you,' she says to Eliza's mum.

'Come and play at my house,' Millie calls to Eliza.

'Maybe another time, Millie,' Laura whispers. Millie must have forgotten. Or she thinks she's going home soon, that they've been on holiday for a week or two.

Today at work, she got an email. He knows she can't close her work email. The threats mostly involved legal action: he would go for full custody, he would go for the house, he would keep everything that was rightfully his. It was couched in such vile terms Laura had to leave her desk, shut herself in the toilet, place her head in her hands and shake. Since leaving, she's felt a little tremor of relief each time she locks something. Even something as simple as a cubicle door. The lock can't really stop anything, but it can close something. Here's a little space I can make my own, for this short length of time.

She shouldn't have opened the email. But if she hadn't, the knowledge of it would have been there in her head all day, eating up her brain. That's what he would have meant it to do. The worst part about it is that he knows it'll get to her, but there's nothing in it she can actually pin on him, no threat of physical violence. She wishes her ex was a stupid arsehole like Karen's, who'd rung up and left death threats on her phone, so Karen went and got a protection order just like that. Craig is a clever arsehole, charming and manipulative. She knows that when it comes to his word against hers, everyone will choose his.

She makes the children sandwiches, pours them each a glass of milk three-quarters full. She sits them at the table. Karen's sons and Ariana's older daughter are in front of the TV again. Laura wishes she could turn it off, but she doesn't want to risk a protest. So she lets Leighton and Millie swivel around in their chairs and stare at the cartoon figures on the screen. At home, they'd have got half an hour of YouTube a day, max. Karen's and Ariana's kids seem to be screen-fixated. Laura wants to throw the TV out the window. It's an old monitor one that would implode in quite a satisfying way when smashed. She wants to go into the bathroom and sit in the shower tray and shred the towels and scream and scream.

Laura boils the jug, makes herself tea, then sees the flowers again. She left them on the table, ignoring them. If I don't look at them, they aren't for me. She places her cup on the bench, lifts them out of the jar someone's stuck them in (Karen?), unlocks the back door and carries them outside. The kids aren't watching. They don't know the flowers were from Dad, anyway. Everything is strange here; they didn't even notice they'd come.

She is surprised by how fast the petals pulp. The weight of her, grinding them into the pimpled slab of concrete. The leaves take longer, but they do shred. She's also surprised by how angry she feels, but no sound comes out. It's a tremendous, powerful, silent anger. She stamps and drives her feet home, rolling the soles of her shoes back and forth, back and forth. It's his head. It's his face. It's the face that leaned over her and didn't care that she was shaking from head to toe. It's the face that looked at her body as if she wasn't in it. She is trashing it. She is pulping it. She is messing it up.

Then Ariana's car turns into the drive, and Laura waves and points at the mushed up bouquet. Ariana grins and runs the remnants over.

Karen has bought some cheap pizzas. 'Friday night, pizza night,' she explains. 'Trying to keep things normal.'

'Oh, yum,' says Ariana.

The table isn't big enough to fit everyone around, and there aren't enough chairs, so the women sit at the table with Leighton and Millie, and the other kids sit in the lounge, plates on their laps. Laura notices the other kids shove food in their mouths without looking. Millie picks out pieces of pineapple and hands them to Laura.

If they were at home, Craig would yell at her, and at Leighton, telling him to sit up and eat properly and stop playing with his food. Telling him to get back here and sit in his chair, stop wiping his hands on the furniture or on the newly waxed floors. Leave your toys and come back to your food or I'll hit you. Leighton's slithered out of his seat and is inching around the back of the armchair where Karen's younger son is sitting. He's peering at the TV, which is showing some dull current affairs show on mute. Laura watches him touch the fabric of the armchair and feels peaceful. No one cares. No one is going to yell. The armchair will absorb everything and keep on sitting in its place, calm and silent.

Millie leaves a picked-clean piece of pizza on her plate. Laura thinks about eating it, but decides against it. Gradually, day by day, she's getting her appetite back. Millie's off outside; it's still light. There's a semi-deflated ball out there and a balance bike that Millie can just fit on with her knees doubled up. The gate is shut, but Laura still feels apprehensive. She clears her plate off the table and follows her daughter outside.

Millie's crouched down next to the house looking at something, completely focused.

'What're you looking at, love?'

Millie looks up at Laura, and grins, and points.

Under the porch there are five kittens: two black, one dark tabby, one light tabby, one black and white. For a while, Laura and Millie watch them together in silence, then Millie runs back inside and shouts out the news.

Everyone wants to see. They leave the TV, they leave their plates, come out the side door and squat down beside the porch. Everyone crowds around to see the kittens: Karen, Ariana, Laura, all seven kids.

'Can we have one, Mum?'

'Can they live in the house?'

'Can we keep them?'

'Can we give them names?'

Laura isn't sure. It's a stray cat. It might have a disease. What if the kittens die?

'I've been feeding her,' Karen confesses. 'Leftovers, and then I got a packet of cat biscuits. I gave her some milk in a saucer. Man, she was hungry.'

'Did she have the kittens last time you saw her?'

'Dunno, I haven't seen her for a day or two.'

Laura remembers the cat wobbling the fence line. When was that? A day ago? Two? Three? All the days blur together. They've been here a week – or is it two? How is one supposed to remember things like days of the week?

'They'll get tame, if we feed them,' Karen says. 'They'll learn to trust us. It might take them a while, but they will.'

The five smallest children are all smooshed up together, busy thinking of names. Whitey-paws. Shadow. Sprinkle. Mighty Cat. Silver. Stripy. Panther. Each sound, once spoken, becoming a possible thing.

The teashop

After a full half hour of whipping the bank manager, Esme lay down beside him on the bed. It was early afternoon, the bank manager's lunch break. The sun cast warm golden squares through the upstairs window. The curtains were drawn back. Anyone in an adjacent upper floor could have looked in, seen Esme treading the bank manager's bottom with her stilettos, seen him writhing with delight. Got all that viewing for free. Well, bugger it, it was worth it for those squares of sun.

Esme did not normally lie on the bed with the clientele, quiet and comfortable like this, but Claude was an old friend. 'Claude,' Esme said, propping herself up on her elbow, 'I think I've fallen in love.'

Claude's bald head was shining. His thick black eyebrows, speckled with grey – silver really, Esme thought – waggled appreciatively.

'Not you, Claude,' Esme said, even though she knew he knew this.

'Tell me who,' he said, picking up her hand and kissing it. 'You have such tiny hands, Esme. For such a hard woman, your hands are so little.'

'Never mind that,' Esme said, pulling her hand away. 'I'm too old to be in love, Claude.'

'A name?'

'His name is Andrew Butters.'

Claude laughed. 'He sounds fat. Is he as fat as me?'

'Possibly fatter.'

'What else is he like?'

'Dull. Sulky.'

'Oh, dull and sulky! That's what you're after?'

Esme smiled to herself, stroking the pink candlewick bedspread. It needed a wash. She would send Patience to the laundrette that afternoon. With the sun, the candlewick, the framed art, the room felt homely, like a grandmother's spare room. In a different life, Esme would have been a grandmother. She was forty-eight, old enough. This is why my men come back, thought Esme. It's restful for them.

'I don't know,' she said to Claude. 'Love is illogical, isn't it?'

Claude laughed again. 'I can't remember.' He had been married for almost thirty years. He'd had plenty of affairs and frequented a number of establishments, the Petunia Teashop being the current favourite. Could it be that he'd forgotten what love was like? Hadn't there been anyone – Linda perhaps, or Lesley – who'd taken his fancy a little more than the others?

'I think I'll marry him,' Esme said. 'If he asks me – and I hope he will.'

'And shut up shop?' Claude looked horrified.

'Oh, no. Prue could competently take over this place. I'll become a proper hausfrau. No makeup. With a kerchief on my head. I'll grow real petunias.'

'I don't believe it.'

Esme sighed. 'What else am I going to do, Claude? Hang around this place until I'm dust and cobwebs? Change the name to Miss Havisham's?'

'I've got a little house in Greytown,' Claude said. 'I'll rent it to you for next to nothing. You can get the Woman Alone pension. You don't have to marry a dull sulk.'

'What on earth would I want to live in Greytown for? I'd rather drink cyanide.'

'Me too,' Claude confessed. 'But, bear it in mind.'

'What if I don't want to be a Woman Alone?' Esme said, as much to the window as to Claude. There was a pigeon on the ledge, a male displaying himself, cooing aggressively. Esme had got to know a lot about pigeons. 'What if I want someone to play chess with by the electric fire, or go for walks in the park with, or go on holidays?'

'With a dull man? Does he have any money?'

'I believe so. Terrible taste in clothes and shoes, a terrible haircut, but he does earn a bit, has a house, and savings. I've been dreaming of catching the train, Claude, going through the South Island, past all those mountains. I'll get some nice new woollen twinsets, and a pair of kitten heels. I'll be like those women in the advertisements, you know, those ones who are just a silhouette on a balcony, with snow in the background.'

'Stop it,' Claude moaned. 'Oh, I can't stand it.' He got up to dress himself. As he stumbled into his underpants, Esme looked at the stripes on his sallow backside. Little by little, she was tanning him. Sooner or later, Claude would be sitting upon pure leather.

'You know, Claude,' Esme said, throwing a robe around her corseted torso, 'I'm telling you all this because I need a job at your bank.'

'I don't have a job for you.'

'No, I expect you don't. But from now on, from several years ago, in fact, if you quite understand me, I work at your bank.'

Claude turned around and winked in recognition. 'I mistrust your motivations.'

'This is very important.' Esme stood against the window so that she might look imposing, dangerous. The sun around her dark hair made a velvet painting of her. 'If anyone comes in and asks to see me, you are to be notified. You are to call Prue. I will be over in ten minutes. You will provide me with whatever uniform your female staff are wearing, which I will keep here. Is all this understood?'

'Oh, yes,' Claude said. 'Quite.' He turned to go, and then paused and shook his head. 'Some marriage this is going to be.'

'It's my only hope.'

Claude saluted her and went downstairs.

Esme met Andrew Butters at three at the Swiss coffee lounge further down Cuba Street. It was newly opened, with pictures of mountains on the walls and waitresses in lacy maid's outfits. Esme saw enough of those at work to feel fatigued just looking at them, but Andrew had chosen the place. His face was flushed, part delight and part embarrassment. They ordered cake and a pot of coffee. Andrew did not take her hand or grope her bottom. He simply sat opposite her, and smiled, and made polite conversation. Yes, thought Esme, I can't expect anyone to understand, but this is really what I want. A boring man. A meat and potatoes man. A man who takes five minutes and goes to sleep, and then the night is mine to breathe in. After all those men who wanted to be spanked, whipped, tied up, stood on, walked on, have things put up their bottoms, or to do those things to somebody else or watch other people do them, a boring man would be like a fresh wind down from the snow.

Andrew talked about his dead wife and his grown-up children.

To have children already grown and not have to carry them and birth them and bring them up. To get an occasional letter from them in the mail, or cook them an occasional Sunday roast. That was the way. Esme drank her coffee, black, and thought about how, at last, things were falling into place. Things would settle, like ornaments on a shelf that were never moved, only dusted. Things must settle; a change of fortune must occur. But that was the gambler's instinct, Esme knew – and a gambler could always lose again. Nine hundred and ninety-nine thousand nine hundred and ninety-nine times out of a million, he would lose again. All of this relied on Claude's cooperation.

Andrew asked her how the bank had been that morning. Esme said it was quiet, things just ticking over. A little like the truth. Mornings generally went that way. She had been sending telexes, she said. The teashop did not have a telex machine, but the bank did. Esme had, on a few occasions, got drunk with Claude after hours and composed filthy abbreviations to various foreign outfits.

When they had finished their cake, Andrew insisted on walking Esme back to work. But it was in the opposite direction from where he was going, Esme said. Not to worry, he would catch the trolley bus back. She should let him. She should let him be the protective gentleman, shield her from the diseased pigeons, the motor exhaust. Esme was trembling all over. She had decades of experience in steeling herself, but it took all her willpower to still her knees, her wrists. She set her shoulders, her breasts pointing out like a pair of torpedoes. Oh, why had she forgotten to change out of that silly brassiere? She would need some new ones, cream coloured, soft, the kind worn by women who are never seen in their underwear, not even by their husbands.

They walked up the footpath side by side in a pleasant silence. For a man like Andrew Butters, walking with a woman in the street was as good as an announcement. A nice woman would not walk with a man she did not intend to marry. Only a common prostitute.

'I very seldom come to this part of town,' Andrew confessed. They crossed at the pedestrian lights, swathes of shoppers, mothers with prams, workmen in overalls around them. The street seemed grimy under Andrew's tasteless but shiny shoes. More pigeons, more litter, fruiterers shouting, a painter in a doorway, smoking. They stopped outside the bank and, to Esme's relief, Andrew did not attempt to walk in with her. People did know her in there, but not as a co-worker. Someone might wink or say something offhand. She would have to remind Claude, tomorrow, to talk to his staff. Andrew did not kiss her goodbye, but gently touched her sleeve. Esme waited until he was out of sight, then crossed the road.

First there was a new girl to deal with and then there were the poets.

The new girl hovered by the counter, looking at the buns. She was thin and looked hungry. The buns were, in fact, fresh that day. Esme had a deal with the bakery three doors down. Now and again, someone really did come in and order tea and cake, someone from out of town perhaps, or an elderly person whose sight was failing. Esme took a bun from under its glass dome, slid it onto a plate and beckoned the girl to a table. Anyone who looked in would see a mother and her daughter, wan and in need of some kind of reprimand. The girl savaged the bun. Esme fetched another, and a lamington. The lamingtons might have been a few days old – possibly mouldy – but this girl looked as though she wouldn't notice.

There were tide marks of makeup around her face, as if she never washed but simply went to bed, got up in the morning and applied a new layer of foundation. How smeary her pillow must be. Esme was reminded of Candice, a former pupil from her schoolmistress days. Perhaps it *was* Candice. Sometimes she recognised girls who came in looking for work. But it had been fifteen, twenty years now. It couldn't be Candice. Perhaps a younger sister. Perhaps even a daughter. The girl didn't look much more than fifteen. Esme's pupils had all genuinely hated her.

'Do you have any experience?' Esme asked.

The girl nodded, choking on a bit of sponge. The word 'experience' meant anything that had brought you through this door. If this girl was anything like the others, it would have been largely unpleasant.

'You will need your own lingerie. Bras, knickers, suspender belts, pantyhose, and at least two corsets. And you will need your own boots. Most of our other costumes are shared.'

The girl nodded.

'Everything is kept clean,' Esme continued, looking at the dust on the glass fruit. Patience must not have bothered that morning. 'If you don't have the right items, I can provide them for you, and subtract the cost from your pay.'

The girl nodded again. 'I don't have anything nice,' she said, starting on the second bun.

'Once you've finished that, we'll go upstairs and measure you.' The bun looked dry. 'Prue, where is the tea?' Esme called.

Prue emerged with a silver pot and two cups. Esme poured one for the girl and watched her scull it.

The poets arrived just as Esme was rolling up her cloth tape-measure and writing down the girl's hips in inches. She was scrawny, but they could fatten her up a bit. Esme had expected to see the poets. They often stopped in at this time of day, freshly drunk.

'A new girl,' the tall poet said.

'She starts on Wednesday,' Esme said, sternly. The girl was putting on her coat.

'Wednesday's child is full of woe,' the short poet murmured.

The tall poet must have been composing something in his head about the girl. He gave her a bloodshot wink. The girl smiled back through the glass of tears. Here was an almost fatherly man, a man she could almost trust. You can't, though, Esme wanted to tell her. He seems all right, this one, he knows how to talk. But he's a thoroughly despicable person.

Instead, she said, 'Wednesday morning, promptly at ten.' The girl answered with a monosyllable and went downstairs. Her shoes were terrible – she would need a new pair of heels. Esme realised she had forgotten to measure her feet.

'Where's that brandy we were drinking last Friday?' the short poet asked, slinging his jacket over a chair. The tall one draped himself across a chaise longue. There were moth holes in his pants. Esme would not offer to darn them. She went to a cupboard and retrieved a bottle. 'Brandy. That could be a good name for her.'

'The new girl? I think Daisy,' said the tall poet.

'Daisy is too prim.'

'Rose, then. A rose is sensuous.'

'But that girl wasn't. Brandy is fine. If she's anything like the rest of them she'll be drunk most of the time.'

'And us.' The short poet smiled. He took out a grubby notebook from his satchel and pressed it open, found a pencil in his trouser pocket. 'Write something,' he said, pushing them at Esme.

She gave him a drink and took the book. 'Write what?'

The pencil still held the warmth of his leg. It was a kind of intimacy.

'Write what you love.'

'What do you mean, what I love?'

'I don't know, just write a list of things.'

'Why?'

'Because I want you to.'

'I don't usually do things men want, if they aren't paying.'

The short poet continued to watch her hands with an expectant smile. He was red-cheeked. He had been on the turps all morning, for sure. Sometimes they had to carry him downstairs, put him on the bench outside the kitchen back door to sober up. He had no home to speak of. There was no one else around.

Esme wrote,

> *Things I love. I love the colour pink. I love hyacinths.*
> *I love violets. I love roses. I love lavender. I love*
> *magnolias. I love the science of botany. I love violins.*
> *I love the sea. I love the twilight. Candles. Bats. A*
> *mountain, covered in snow. The whistle of a train.*
> *I love real teashops. Cream horns. French crêpes*
> *sprinkled with sugar. I love hot baths. I love new*
> *leather, the smell of it. I love my love . . .*

'That last line isn't original,' said the short poet, peering over her shoulder.

Esme slapped the book down on the three-legged table. 'No, it isn't. But it's true.'

'Do you really love somebody?' the tall poet asked, languorously.

'Yes.'

'Is it me?'

'No it isn't.'

'We have no money today, etcetera,' said the short poet.

Esme looked out the window. It was impossible to tell if it would rain or not. She would feel it, walking home. *The sound of rain on an umbrella. A wet footpath shining in the streetlights. Lighted doors. The florist shop's window display. The cheerful florist, who hates no one* – but that was an assumption. The florist may have had her hates. Every morning she swept outside her door and smiled like the world was made anew. But that in itself may have been window-dressing. All flowers grow out of dirt.

The professor was married. Esme was nineteen. At the end of her second year at university, she'd signed up for a summer job as a research assistant. They were working on the fern section of a new complete description of New Zealand flora.

'I was expecting a boy,' the professor said.

'I can work as well as a boy,' Esme said, matter-of-factly. She wore plain, sensible clothes, had her hair cut in a daring bob. 'I've been tramping lots of times. I'm very fit.'

The professor looked at her breasts, blossoming under her white blouse. Esme did not wear a corset. 'You'll do,' he said.

Esme, the professor, two doctors and another male research assistant set up their canvas tents in a grassy place by the forest. The men went in the big tent. The professor said Esme would have to sleep in the small tent by herself for her own safety. The first night, he walked over, pulled apart the tent flaps and unzipped her sleeping bag. It was painful, quick and disappointing. The next day, walking through the bush, Esme hurt with every step. It was a kind of dry, rough hurt, like there was something wooden and splintery stuck inside her. When she stopped to urinate, and wiped herself with a leaf, there was a dark smear of blood on it. She trailed the professor through carpets of filmy ferns, collecting specimens for the leaf press. The doctors and the other assistant largely ignored her.

The professor had fine sandy hair, a slightly receding hairline. He wore shorts and hiking boots with long woollen socks. They had a complicated diamond pattern. Esme wondered if his wife had knitted them. She was a terrible knitter, herself. Terrible cook, terrible seamstress. She did not like being indoors. She wanted to work there, forever, in the forest. While the professor was on his hands and knees in the undergrowth, Esme saw there were tiny white flowers caught in his hair. She pulled one out with her thumb and middle finger. The professor, not looking up, batted her hand away. She looked at the flower up close: purple on the inside with minute stamens like short, snipped threads. She knew all the Latin names of the plants, all the terms for flower parts. She knew their life cycles, she knew their orders. She could draw specimens better than any of the other students. She watched the other assistant making messy hairs with his pencil. His hand hovered as if he wasn't sure what shape to make. His notebook was full of scrawls. In the evenings they sat side by side, drawing, writing things down, not speaking to each other. Perhaps the young man was shy, or perhaps he thought Esme was beneath him.

The second evening the professor gave her his boots and a brush and, without word, she cleaned them. That night, another fuck in the tent, this time less painful. 'God, you're so beautiful,' the professor said. He had not looked at her all day. 'Look at you. My god.' But how could she look at herself? Was he, in fact, talking to an unseen creator? Esme did not believe in anything. When the professor went back to the men's tent to sleep, she was cold. There were strange calls in the forest: some birds she knew, some she didn't. They started singing early in the morning, thrashing the air with their shrill territorial displays. Esme took the billy and some water from the stream, made porridge, burned it on the bottom, was reprimanded. The air was so cold up there in the mountains. The campfire made her eyes water.

Esme could not tell Andrew why she found the gorilla so funny. It was because he reminded her of Claude, with his big brows and leathery bottom. He sat there in his cage, mutely scratching himself. There was a limp pile of lettuce in his dish.

'He looks lonely,' Andrew observed.

'He does,' said Esme through her laughter. 'We must ask the zoo to buy him a lady gorilla.' Then she laughed again, and the gorilla must have caught a glimpse of her teeth, because he got to his feet, walked to the bars and grimaced at them. Andrew put his arm in front of her, instinctively. 'Let's have a look at the elephant,' Esme suggested, and hoped it wouldn't remind her of anyone.

On Saturdays she did not open until four. Today she had taken the evening off and left Prue in charge. She and Andrew walked around the zoo until her feet were tired, pinched in her shoes, and then they ate at the tearooms. A parrot was screaming in the background. The sun was shining, and the seats were not uncomfortable, and the sandwiches were good and fresh, but the scream cut through everything, made Esme's head hurt. They caught the trolley bus back through town, and then the cable car, and Esme invited Andrew into her flat for tea.

It was a modest home, but clean. Upstairs was the bathroom and bedroom, downstairs the kitchen and a small parlour with two armchairs, a mahogany table, a fringed floor lamp. Esme put out cheese and pickles, some boiled eggs, some bread. Halfway through a slice, Andrew left his chair and kneeled on the floor. He told her she was the woman he had hoped to meet since his wife died. She was unpretentious. She was a good listener. Most of all, she was a virtuous woman – he could see that. She had never been married but had kept her virtue. She did not disgrace herself in her work. She would not need to work anymore. They would spend the remainder of their lives together.

It still wasn't clinched, Esme thought that night, alone in bed. Something could still spoil it. Perhaps he would notice she dyed her hair – it wasn't naturally so black. Perhaps she had laughed too hard at the gorilla. She might still be discovered.

The professor told her he had decided to stay with his wife. This was untrue. He had never considered leaving her. There had not been a decision to make. He and Esme would not be lovers anymore.

He told her, furthermore, that she would never be a scientist. She would get married soon and become a mother and then she would be too busy washing nappies and sterilising bottles to think about plants. If she wanted to work, she might find something as a schoolmistress. She might teach Domestic Science at the local girls' school.

The professor told her that a woman as fast as her had better get married as quickly as she could, before it was too late. He told her she was a slut and a whore, and he had never really loved her. He had said he did, but only because lust had confused him. Men did not love sluts.

Esme went down to the sea and jumped off the wharf. She swam out as far as she could. The cold got into her muscles and stiffened them. Her arms slowed down, could hardly push against the rise and fall of the waves. She began to choke on gulps of seawater. She remembered reading that drowning was very painful. But it couldn't possibly be more painful than being alive.

A little fishing launch pulled her out. The skipper expected some kind of reward. Esme had lost her purse, and what little money she had in it, in the sea. Ashore, stripped naked and wrapped in a fishy-smelling blanket, she sucked the fisherman's cock. He ejaculated in her hair. When he had gone, she walked down the wharf, climbed down a ladder into the water and washed it out. Salt and sand stung her eyes; ropes of snot poured from her nose. She shook in great jerks. She thought about trying again. She clutched handfuls of the seaweed that clung to the ladder and shivered and lost her nerve.

'Don't marry him,' Claude said.

'Well, I can't marry you,' Esme said. 'You're already married.'

'I don't need reminding.' Claude was looking for his cigarette case, slumped over, forcing his belly into turgid rolls.

Men never care about angles, Esme thought.

'You'll die of boredom.'

'Perhaps I want to. I'd rather die of boredom than starvation.'

'You aren't going to starve,' Claude scoffed. It wasn't what she meant. It was spiritual starvation as much as physical. This was a place one simply could not grow old in.

'Don't marry him,' said Claude again. 'Pass me that matchbox.' He was pathetic, really pathetic. He did not love her: he needed her, in some infantile way. There were probably psychoanalysts who could unravel Claude in about three minutes. He lit his cigarette and leaned back on the pile of pillows propped against the headboard. His bare chest and belly were covered in thick black hair. He really is disgusting, thought Esme. Just like the gorilla. They are all disgusting.

'Prue will run a tight ship,' Esme said. 'Everything will keep ticking over. You'll keep coming here.'

'Prue's an old stick insect. She's a tree wētā. You're my ideal woman – tall, curvy, fat-bottomed . . .'

'Stop it.' Esme opened the window a chink. The smoke was making her dizzy.

'I'll report you. I'll have the place shut down.'

'You wouldn't.'

'I would.'

'You're an arsehole, Claude.' She knew he wouldn't. The thing was, she did not love Andrew Butters. Claude was right. It was all meaningless in the end. 'I'm getting married in December. Prue will run a Christmas special after I finish up. Nuns, angels, Virgin Marys, all things bright and beautiful.'

'Oh, shut up about Prue. And bugger Christmas.'

'So,' Esme went on, as if he hadn't spoken, 'I will need that job at the bank for another two months. Two months is all I am asking. Don't stuff up my life, Claude. God knows I know enough about you to stuff up yours.'

A teacher goes into the cupboard at night with the brooms. A teacher is an object of general revulsion. No one would ever want to make love to a teacher. She is a warning to girls of what they might become if they play their cards wrong. A dehydrated tortoise with a searching neck or a fat, furtive lesbian. She wears long skirts and several petticoats and smells of chalk. She is a repository of dead dreams. After the professor refused to accept Esme as a master's student, she went to training college. She began teaching at the age of twenty-one. Then, already, she knew she was ancient, finished, had it, an old maid, a spinster, wrecked, lost, ruined. The girls would sit before her in their gym frocks, with their smooth skin and pink cheeks, gloating. We are fifteen, they seemed to sing in chorus. We are the ones all the poems are written about. We are the ones in the films. We are pressed into every new record. We replace ourselves every year. All you can do is recede into the night before us. They spilled ink; they screwed up little balls of paper and threw them at her. They passed rude notes, drew caricatures in their notebooks, labelled them 'Science Mistress'. Sometimes she had snake teeth, sometimes a fork and pointed tail. She wanted to round all the girls up and sell them. Put them on a boat to go and work in some foul foreign port. She walked between her boarding house and her workplace. She became a ghost that floated across the blackboard, a skeleton wearing a dull flesh suit. All the staff in the school were women. The city – a town, really – was small enough that everybody knew about the professor. And the doctor the following year. If it weren't for her immorality, she may have become a scientist, people said. She had something of a talent for botanical drawing. But after all, she is a woman. To a woman, flowers are for decoration.

Esme was found on the roof of the assembly hall with her shoes and socks off, feet resting in the gutter. She had no recollection of how she had got there. She was dismissed on account of being unfit to teach. On the recommendation of the headmistress, she went into a hospital for the insane. She was kept there for a few months, dressed in shapeless white. Everything was white: walls, tiles, bedsheets, the steel-framed beds, the weird headgear of the nurses. No one came to see her. There was nothing to do. Esme found she could avoid the worst of it by sitting quietly, saying nothing and being courteous to the doctors. Things went badly for the noisy ones.

One night a young schizophrenic went into a rage, and while the nurses were preoccupied, Esme climbed out through a window and onto the streets of Newtown.

In a lane behind a pub, which was shut, she came across a middle-aged woman in a shawl, skirts hitched, warming her cunt over a fire. The woman was singing to herself, drawing circles in the air with her pelvis. Esme had never felt anything like what she felt watching this demon of the night.

'Where have you come from?' the woman asked her. Esme told her. 'I've got a job for you,' the woman said.

Esme neared the fire and held out her hands over the coals. They did not throw much heat.

'You look cold,' said the woman. 'Take my shawl, I don't need it.' She wrapped it around Esme's shoulders like a spider wrapping its breakfast. The woman went by the name of Madame Columba. She had a house on Adelaide Road. Esme could start there the following day.

'The funny farm will never find you,' Madame Columba said. 'I have some good friends in the psychiatric department.'

Esme walked from her flat, down past Parliament and along Lambton Quay. She watched the wind lift a bowler hat, and a man chase it and catch it with a stamp of his foot. Triumphant, he held it up, unflattened it and replaced it on his head. It would have cost a few bob, Esme thought, as she nodded to a civil servant on her right. His face looked familiar, though she couldn't quite pick it. In her drab beige coat, she could pass for a secretary. A few yards on, another hat went flying. Bowlers rolled well. One had to have a hat, but so did the wind. The wind made a mess of her hair, scraped wisps from her topknot. A sheet of newspaper, come loose from a bundle of chips, was swirling in the air like a kite.

Esme liked to walk to work. It helped keep the calves shapely, helped stop one's brain from rotting. The woollen coat made her feel a little like a camel. The city was the desert. Once she arrived at the teashop – her oasis, of sorts – she would hang the coat up and wrap a black shawl around her shoulders: Madame Columba's shawl. The crochet so fine, the yarn so strong, it had lasted all these years. Soon it would be someone else's turn to be Madame Columba. Our Lady of the Pigeons.

At the front door Esme found Prue waiting, sour-faced. It was not that Esme had deliberately kept her waiting – she was always punctual – but that Prue was too early, as usual. She had a roof over her head at nights, nowadays, but the place she was living got noisy in the mornings, the kitchen too full.

The key made its reassuring click in the lock; the door swung in, tingling its brass bell. There was that stale baked-goods smell and, from elsewhere in the building, something like incense, smoke, and another note – something dark and inescapable. Was it merely the old building, ancient sarking, a taint of creosote? The skin of thousands floated into the loops of worn carpets? Or did people's own thoughts have a scent? Esme only knew she was sick of it, sick to the core. She smelled it every night, late, when she went to sleep.

There were Prue's spindly hands, lugging the sandwich board outside.

'Prue, file your nails when you've finished with that,' Esme said. 'They look ragged. And,' she added, feeling the cruelty of it, but unable to resist, 'do something about your cheeks.' She couldn't very well say 'face'. Prue couldn't help that. Prue clattered out the door, giving a tiny nod of assent – or was it resignation?

The thing was, Esme said to Prue as they went over the cashbook, things always had a way of turning out badly. You went from one failure to the next. The trick was to get out before things got too awful. 'I don't want to be the old woman gyrating over a fire in a back alley,' she said.

Prue gave her customary nod. Esme had told her that story innumerable times. She couldn't remember exactly what had happened, or when. Perhaps Madame Columba had given her the shawl that night, or perhaps it had been weeks or even years later, when she was working at her Ruby Palace. The first Madame Columba – or had she been the second, third or hundredth? – was certainly dead now.

From the street below came the sound of singing. Perhaps it was the florist. 'Shut the window,' Esme said. 'I have a headache.'

'The thing is, Prue,' she went on, squaring a pile of pound notes, 'if I stay in this place, it will roast me alive.' It sounded ridiculous, but it did feel like a great lamp, or a grill, came down over her from time to time. 'Do you remember Oranges and Lemons? The bit where it says, "Here comes a chopper to chop off your head"?' It was like that, here comes a chopper. She was always dodging the chopper.

'You know something,' said Prue. 'It does cheer me up, to give them a good whacking.'

'I used to feel that way,' Esme said.

Esme was making up a bed when she heard Prue's little feet clatter up the stairs. The brown wiry face – tree wētā was cruel – popped around the doorframe. 'A gentleman here to see you.'

'Me?' Esme walked into the anteroom. Gentlemen were not to come in and simply ask to see her. Only a select few saw her. Prue knew that. The rest took their pick of the girls. There were two of them mooching on the couch right now, and another in the bathroom. Surely –

'He asked specifically for a mature woman,' Prue said, with careful emphasis. Was Prue insulting her? After all these years Esme had kept her off the street? Esme felt her temper beginning to flare. Prue could do it herself.

'He also asked for a proper hiding. Says he's been wicked.'

'They all say that,' Esme muttered. 'If he wants to see Madame C he can pay double.'

'Righto,' Prue said, and went back downstairs.

In less than a minute, she returned. 'Oh, you should see this one.' She laughed. She'd forgotten, or forgiven, Esme's anger. 'You'll have fun with him.'

'Bring him up and I will see him in ten minutes.'

Patience emerged from the bathroom in a pink slip with fur trim, with a towel on her head. An old towel, too. 'Take off that towel and go and dry your hair properly, my girl,' Esme snapped. Patience blinked. Esme went back into the room with the freshly made bed, closing the door behind her.

She heard Prue's footsteps again, with a heavy tread ascending behind her, and felt the shift in the air that meant a male was there. She heard one of the girls giggling. She took off her clothes, looked at her long white naked body in the wardrobe mirror. Soon, she would be married, and all this would be no more. She took a leather corset from the wardrobe, drew the laces tight until her ribs contorted and her breasts were a soft pillow under her chin. She pulled her boots on, laced them furiously, touched up her lip liner, made a venomous face at herself in the glass.

Then she knew what would happen – she was sure of it. It was the event she had been dreading, that she'd felt in her belly like a clump of swallowed tacks. It would be him, Andrew. He would be like all those other men: a steadfast husband in one life, an insatiable lech in another. He would be sitting there in the armchair in the anteroom with a dull, stupid look on his face, and he would look up and see her, his bride-to-be, bursting out of her leather, and he would know who she was. His face would collapse. He would pick up his briefcase and walk out. She would never hear from him again. She would turn into a skeleton in a closet.

And she knew she did love him, after all. *Because I know my love loves me.* Stupid, stupid of her to risk that.

Esme heard Prue say, 'She'll be with you in a moment.' The corset stunted her breath. Downstairs, or perhaps in an adjacent building, she heard a door slam as if the wind had caught it. It was a door closing on her. She knew it was. She could not go back out there. She stood in the bedroom and tried to breathe.

Esme went to the window, looked out and saw the grimy street, and the pigeons, and the dry leaves blowing, and the florist crossing the road with something in a bucket.

A quiet death

The sky is a beautiful dove grey. A soft colour, almost blue. It is soothing, with my eyes open, looking at the sky. It is as though the sky is bathing my eyes.

Something is strange about the sky. Or is it something strange about the window, or the standard-issue curtains? Or this room, where I have been lying in this bed, all tubed up, for a week. Or thereabouts. Each morning I have woken up, the sky outside the window has been different, but I haven't counted the mornings. Someone must have opened the curtain, walking in soft-soled shoes. The nurse never wakes me: I wake to find myself alone, lying here in the usual amount of pain, with this view before me. The ceiling tiles with their pattern of holes.

Then I realise what is wrong with the sky: I am not supposed to be seeing it. Holy actual fuck. This is not what was intended.

It should have happened last night. I said goodbye to them, held their hands. Susan had her arms around me for a long time. I cupped each child's face in my palms, kissed their foreheads, said, 'Mummy loves you.' They didn't want to stay in the room and see me go. When I fell asleep, they left. It was going to happen peacefully while I slept, some time during the hours of darkness. Quiet, painless.

But there is the sky, grey, shapeless. There are clouds I can't quite make out without glasses, but I know they are there: different tones, cumulus forms.

And it occurs to me that I want this. I want to keep on waking up every morning. I want to open my eyes and see the colour of the sky from my own bed, my bed at home, the bed that smells right. See uncertain birds moving across the sky.

Even with my stomach unable to hold food, I want to breathe in the smell of cooking from down the hall.

I want to lie dying in my home, with my wine-red blanket and the big naked painting of Susan on the wall opposite the bed. I want to watch the sun moving across the room little by little, hear the house sighing in the heat and the breeze, have my children come into the room and kiss me beside the tube in my nose and read to me, even if I can't focus on the words.

There is sound in the room, and I realise there's someone in here with me. The doctor is moving around. He's preparing something next to the bed. Well, that can be clarified. I will be going home.

'Oh, you're awake,' he says.

Clearly, I've been moved down the to-do list. He was busy in the night: emergencies, unforeseen events. Well, that works out fine for me, because I have changed my mind. I've had the counselling and signed every form there is to sign, and it's all been done to the correct timeframe, and to the letter of the law, but I have changed my mind, and I reserve the right to change my mind.

'I've decided against this,' I tell the doctor, trying to focus on his general shape.

Is my voice incoherent? Has he not registered that I am speaking? Can it be possible that he is ignoring me and carrying out his task regardless?

It occurs to me that there should be someone else on hand. He could at least have asked me if I'd like to see the chaplain, although I've told him a hundred times I'm an atheist. People convert on their death beds; I might have wanted to. There should also be a nurse present. I should have been able to ask for a female nurse, like in the years when our family couldn't get a female doctor, and every time Susan or I went in for something womanly we'd ask to have a nurse present. No man was going to fumble with us alone behind closed doors.

The doctor takes a syringe from a little tray on the bedside cabinet, finds a vein.

'I've changed my mind,' I say.

The needle moves towards me.

'I've changed my mind.' He still hasn't heard me, or he's still ignoring me. It's like in a nightmare, when you try to call out, like you're a small child calling to your parents, but sleep paralysis has you by the throat and no sound comes out.

I gather all my strength in my feeble vocal cords. Air fills my lungs. 'I've CHANGED MY MIND,' I shout. But is it shouting? Can I even shout anymore? 'STOP! I DON'T WANT YOU TO DO THIS!'

The doctor's hand steadies me. The needle goes in.

I am walking down a carpeted corridor towards a set of doors. They swing open on their hinges, and I enter an auditorium. It's massive and dark. It is body-warm like a womb, comfortingly dim. As my eyes accustom to the low light, I look around and see rows and rows of women. They are all women. I think I hear the rustle of paper, the movement of feet. A show is about to start.

I see my fourth-form maths teacher and my mother's best friend, and my best friend's mother, and the writer who won that prize and then had to say goodbye to her children.

Why are all these women gathered here? And why am I among them?

The only thing I know they have in common is that they are no longer. I don't know all of them, but I know this. They are photographs smiling on mantelpieces, saved newspaper clippings, obituaries. They are all filed in the past. I see faces turn to me. I think I can hear a low voice saying 'Welcome'. It is the kind of voice that, all my life, whenever I heard it, reassured me. It is my mother's voice, or my grandmother's. Then it fades out, sound fades out, and colour, and a paleness resumes. I am no longer in the auditorium with the women. I am suspended, for the time being, from joining them in their waiting.

In the hospital room my body lies on the bed. It doesn't seem strange to me that I am standing here, witnessing my body. I lived in it for forty-four years.

The doctor has removed my tubes. He has removed my gown. My shell is still. I don't understand why he is inspecting it like this. They knew exactly what was wrong with me – the size of the tumours and where. He's filled in the requisite piece of paper with the time and cause of death. It's sitting on a clipboard on the ugly Melteca cabinet beside the bed.

It was my cause for a long time. I went around the neighbourhood with petitions, I went to rallies, I wrote to politicians. I wasn't going to have my children see me suffer. I was going to do this with dignity. I wanted it to be my choice. When the referendum came in on my side, I was jubilant. The law changed. Everything felt peaceful and possible.

The doctor unzips himself and parts the legs of my body. He fingers my cunt, deep, deeper. He rubs his semi-erect penis up and down the insides of my thighs, swelling and stiffening himself. He bends down and puts his tongue in my cunt. He licks me frantically, chews on my labia and clitoris. That would have hurt. His hands are wrenching my stomach, the spaces where my breasts were. He puts one finger, then two, then three, into my anus, pokes deep into my bowels. In my insides, the bacteria that have helped me so many years will be moving onto their next job, turning me back into earth. But I will be cremated. The funeral's Saturday. I planned the whole thing, like a wedding. I designed a pamphlet, picked out a poem, made an order of service, asked people to speak, told them the kinds of things I hoped they'd say, made a track list. Some people asked me not to talk about it. Others were understanding. I had developed a facial expression that I always used when discussing my funeral: what I thought was a calm, resolved smile. Dear friend, dear family member – do not be sad for me. My life has been wonderful.

Well, fuck. I don't want a funeral anymore.

That woman, Susan's friend the shaman. I forget her name. I was never sure whether she and Susan were having an affair. Well, I couldn't blame Susan – if your wife was undergoing chemo, and her hair had all fallen out, and her skin was pale, and her voice was dry and croaky, of course you'd look at the women around you who were living, who were resplendent with life in all its colours and smells and tastes. You'd look for a woman whose body hadn't been savaged by disease and surgery, who wasn't pumped full of poison to keep her gasping through a few more months or years. That woman, who never wore a bra and had a penchant for seventies florals. Whole wardrobes full of maxi dresses, dark-coloured fabrics with flower patterns, like a meadow by a folktale forest, long black hair in a loose plait down to her arse. Stinking of some smoky, musky perfume. Susan was always into New Agey stuff. She talked to me about it when it came time to decide how I'd go.

I was a sceptic. I didn't believe in any of Susan's superstitious stuff: astrology, acupuncture, the tarot, reiki, crystals, bogus whitewashed Hinduism, homeopathy. She'd wanted me to try some kind of alternative healing, or several kinds. I said to her, Susan, there is a name for alternative medicines that have been shown to work, and that is 'medicines'. When we were done with talking about healing and were talking about dying, Susan said her friend had done shamanic training and could be there with me. She could say some spells, burn oils. No, I said, I have no problem with the medical establishment. I could picture Susan's friend now, drifting through the hallways, her bare feet with their annoying tinkling anklets padding over the bricks in the courtyard. Oh, to be in my home and see the sun shining on those bricks, and the little weeds – shepherd's purse, fumitory, purslane, scarlet pimpernel – I could never keep from growing there. If I could be home with my babies, and with Susan sitting in the chair beside my bed, holding my hand, stroking my hand the way she used to, I wouldn't mind having that woman there. After my last op she'd been hanging around, helping Susan with the kids and the cooking and the housework. The house smelled of different food, but perhaps that was just because my sense of smell was mangled. Tricia – that was her name, now I remember. Tricia brought me marijuana, to help with my appetite. I couldn't smoke it – one puff on her pipe and I was coughing, choking, until I thought she was trying to kill me. So she got an old saucepan and melted butter with buds, stinking out the house, and baked a batch of wholemeal chocolate brownies. I have never tasted anything so good. I ate two brownies and lay there, body stoned, in a state of bliss. I was the happiest I had ever been.

I would gladly lie now and have Tricia lay her many-ringed hands on me, mutter meaningless and non-specific incantations, and chant me through my death, with the wailing and gnashing of teeth and the incense and beads and cultural appropriation. And have her say that death is magical, that it is purposeful.

As the doctor puts his cock in my dry, dead cunt, breathing hard, I realise no one will check for evidence. This man has performed his assigned tasks. He has filled out the forms. There should have been someone else in the room. There is not. He knows where the other staff are. Or he doesn't – the thrill of possibly being caught violating a dead woman is part of the turn-on. I watch his facial muscles flicker with pleasure as he thrusts faster and faster. He makes small noises of urgent joy. The hospital bed rolls on its wheels, in time with his motions. He is joyously fucking my corpse. He has the cheeks of my bottom in his hands, he is dragging me at him, over and over. His lips move as he speaks to me under his breath. No one will test the semen he is going to shoot into my body, find his DNA there. No one will even think to look for it. I'll be wrapped in a shroud after this, taken to the morgue, collected by my family, placed in an eco-friendly cardboard coffin that the children have decorated with their wobbly worlds, their creatures of dreams.

Young, before kids, Susan and I walked through the galleries and museums of London, Paris, Brussels, Florence, Dresden. Sandalled, hand in hand, we looked at masterpieces. We looked at stolen artefacts. We looked at a history of pigments. We looked at cherubs and madonnas. We looked at centuries of the art of rape. The rape of Lucretia. The rape of Proserpina. The rape of Leda. The rape of Helen. The rape of Cassandra. The rape of the Sabine women. I can't remember where it was, where I was distracted by something – checking the time on my phone, perhaps, thinking about trains. And I can't remember the exact image that upset Susan. But I heard a low cry and looked over, and saw her face contorted in agony. Her whole face, drawn into round lines; her wide open, crying mouth in the middle; her teeth shuddering; her eyes streaming. Susan could not prevent herself from audibly sobbing in the gallery. I went to her and hugged her tightly, gathered her face into my traveller's cotton shawl so that no one else in the room could see those lines of grief. Because it was not theirs to view; it was not a public display – it was Susan's own, personal grief. We made our way silently through the maze of white walls and corridors, down the grand marble staircases of whatever repository of culture we were in. We walked past dead lobsters and luminous grapes, vase upon vase of flowers. We walked past the sun and the moon and gods and wars and sailing ships. We came out the entrance into the sunshine, and I glanced at the expensive ticket in my trouser pocket and a small part of me wondered if I had seen that many euros' worth of art that day. But that didn't matter: what mattered was Susan, and that Susan, who was shaking all over as she sat on a bench in the sunshine, was all right.

Susan sat in the sun with me and cried for about an hour and a half. I honestly do not know how I have forgotten our surroundings so entirely. But I remember suggesting we find some food, and Susan agreed.

In the evening, in the hotel, as she was brushing her hair and soaking her feet in a bucket of tepid water, she said, 'It's just that it brings it all back, for me.'

'I know,' I said.

'And suddenly I feel like I'm drowning.'

'Yeah, I know.'

'Like I can't breathe. Like however much time goes past, he will always be there, doing that to me, and it takes all my willpower to keep that out of my mind.'

I sat with my arm around her.

'I am so tired,' she told me, looking at her feet.

'It's okay,' I said. 'You're allowed to be tired. We are all so tired, aren't we, Susan? We're all so tired of this shit.' But I knew in some way that Susan was more tired than I was. It didn't do to compare one's experiences, but for Susan, who would sometimes forget herself completely, who would look around her and think, Who am I and how did I get here? who would be paralysed from time to time with panic, who would accidentally read an article online and then have to go to bed for the day – for Susan it was quite, quite shit. More shit than it was for me.

I thought that maybe the museums of modern art would be better. That there would be more women artists in them. Maybe we had picked the wrong month, but there seemed to be a distinct shortage. And there were those tidy cards, written in serious curatorial tones, about masculinity and power and violence and sex, and I thought that perhaps what men wanted to do to women was cut us up. It made no sense to me at all. That people would argue for a biological basis for sexual violence, but here they were, saying what they really wanted was to completely destroy us. In destroying the female body, weren't we all destroying ourselves? I was in a philosophical tunnel, like a Möbius strip, going around and around endlessly. Susan became allergic to visual art for quite some time.

We returned home and realised we had survived the trip, our relationship intact. We figured, given that, we'd survive anything. We got married. We filled in all the forms, we went to counselling, we went through all the hoops, we found a donor, we had the kids. First Susan, then me, then Susan again. Bodies grew inside our bodies and emerged out of them, and screamed, and fed, and grew. They had names, grew hair and teeth, learned to walk, to talk, to call us 'Mummy' and 'Mum-Mum'. They learned to draw, and drew us and themselves, all kinds of colours and shapes. Together, the five of us were an intact world, an inviolable world.

And then I got cancer. My body turned on itself, and I was cut up.

I haven't been with a man sexually for nineteen years. I've been with a bunch of women, and then lived monogamously with Susan for sixteen of those years. Being fucked by a man did very little for me at any time. It can't, of course, do anything for me now. All I can do is stand in the room and watch as the doctor climaxes with a loud, low moan, and with a last 'Huh!' pumps in his load. There. My body – my scarred, cancerous woman's body – is fully defiled. Both my breasts cut off, empty pouches. My womb, ovaries, fallopian tubes cut out. I had thought of my body as a generic, androgynous body. It isn't. The doctor lies over me for a few moments, pressing himself into me as he softens, enjoying the feeling of his warm, live wetness inside my deadness. Then he pulls out, wipes himself, zips himself up and gathers his belongings as if nothing has happened. He walks past me without a word.

The sky is still the same colour. The colour of the dress I wore when I married Susan. She wore yellow, like yolk, like the sun.

I am moving out of the room. I find myself walking down the same carpeted corridor. Fluorescent lights zing around me. I have to get out of this light place and back to that dark place. The warm and welcoming place, the rustling place, the voices murmuring, welcoming me in. All I can do now is go there. All I can do is go and take my place among the women.

Acknowledgements

This work was completed with the help of a grant from Creative New Zealand.

The Aotea Ora trust on Great Barrier Island / Aotea generously supported me with an artist's residency in 2019. Thanks for the once-in-a-lifetime experience.

Thanks to Damien Wilkins, Harry Ricketts and Fergus Barrowman for your initial encouragement and support for this project.

Thanks to the VUP team, especially Jasmine Sargent, who is an excellent editor.

Thanks to the editors of the publications and websites where some of these stories have previously appeared: *Sport, Turbine, Hue and Cry, Penduline, Landfall, VUP Home Reader,* Newsroom.

Thanks to the first readers of these stories for offering helpful feedback: Maria McMillan, Carly Thomas, Anna Smaill, Allan Drew, Angela Andrews, Sue Orr and Michalia Arathimos.

Whitney, Cass and Holly – Thanks for writing with me on Wednesdays and sharing your lounges with me.

To the Brilliant and Amazing Writers and Mothers – Thanks for being a supportive online community and for listening and giving advice on writing, reading and all kinds of other things.

Thanks to my beloved friends and family who have supported me over the years I have been working on this collection. It's been possible because of you.